ABBY AND THE
NOTORIOUS NEIGHBOR

**Other books by
Ann M. Martin**

*P.S. Longer Letter Later
(written with Paula Danziger)
Leo the Magnificat
Rachel Parker, Kindergarten Show-off
Eleven Kids, One Summer
Ma and Pa Dracula
Yours Turly, Shirley
Ten Kids, No Pets
Slam Book
Just a Summer Romance
Missing Since Monday
With You and Without You
Me and Katie (the Pest)
Stage Fright
Inside Out
Bummer Summer*

THE KIDS IN MS. COLMAN'S CLASS series
BABY-SITTERS LITTLE SISTER series
THE BABY-SITTERS CLUB mysteries
THE BABY-SITTERS CLUB series
CALIFORNIA DIARIES series

ABBY AND THE
NOTORIOUS NEIGHBOR

Ann M. Martin

AN
APPLE
PAPERBACK

SCHOLASTIC INC.
New York Toronto London Auckland Sydney

Cover art by Ed Acuña

No part of this publication may be reproduced in whole or in part, or stored in a retrieval system, or transmitted in any form or by any means, electronic, mechanical, photocopying, recording, or otherwise, without written permission of the publisher. For information regarding permission, write to Scholastic Inc., Attention: Permissions Department, 555 Broadway, New York, NY 10012.

ISBN 0-590-05975-0

12 11 10 9 8 7 6 5 4 3 2 1   8 9/9 0 1 2 3/0

Printed in the U.S.A.   40
First Scholastic printing, June 1998

*The author gratefully acknowledges
Ellen Miles
for her help in
preparing this manuscript.*

CHAPTER 1

"Ahh . . . ahhh . . . ahhh — CHOO!"

"Bless you." My mom looked up from her newspaper. "You've been sneezing a lot this morning, haven't you?"

"Twedy-dide tibes sidce I woke up," I said, nodding. "A record eved for be." I wiped my streaming eyes with a napkin and reached for a cinnamon roll.

"You sound awful!" said Anna, my twin sister. (Even though we're identical, she doesn't have any allergies. I have enough for both of us, a fact I may just have to hold against her until we're eighty.)

"I feel biserable," I admitted. I did, too. My nose was totally stuffed up, my head was aching, and my throat felt scratchy. Not to mention my brain, which felt as if it were wrapped in cotton. I didn't know how I was going to make it through a whole day at school.

1

It was a Monday morning in early June, which meant that I wouldn't have to worry about making it through too many more days of school. Classes were winding down, which was good. Allergy season was winding up, which was very, very bad.

My name's Abby Stevenson, and I'm allergic to just about everything in the universe: dust, shellfish, milk, pollen, dogs. Not cats, though, believe it or not. I am, however, allergic to kitty litter. Go figure, as a New Yorker might say. I know New Yorkese because I'm originally from Long Island. I just moved here ("here" is Stoneybrook, Connecticut) recently. Anna and I are thirteen and in the eighth grade at Stoney-brook Middle School, otherwise known as SMS.

We've made plenty of new friends. Anna's are mostly kids she knows from music classes, since her life pretty much revolves around her violin (she's an awesome fiddler). Mine are either teammates (I'm kind of a jock) or members of this great club I belong to (the Baby-sitters Club, or BSC — more about that later). None of our new pals has any trouble telling my twin and me apart, even though we have identical genes. We never dress alike, for one thing, and while we both have thick, curly brown hair, I wear mine long and Anna's is cut short, with bangs. We're both nearsighted, though, and always wear either glasses or contacts.

That morning, I was wearing my glasses. I hadn't worn contacts for days, since my eyes had been way too itchy. In fact, my eyes were so teary now that I had to take off my glasses to wipe them again. Then I sneezed, for the thirtieth time since I'd woken up. After the sneeze, I coughed a little. My throat was feeling scratchier by the minute.

My mother looked up again, and concern showed in her eyes. "I wish I didn't have a late meeting today," she said. "I don't like the way that cough sounds." My mom worries about me a bit, because along with the allergies I also have asthma, which, when I have attacks, leaves me gasping for air. I can usually control the asthma with my prescription inhalers. But a couple of times I've had really bad attacks that landed me in the ER. Scary.

"I'll be fide," I said. While I don't always love the hours my mom keeps — she's a high-powered editor at a New York publishing house — I know her job means a lot to her, and I didn't want her to skip an important meeting. "I took by bedicide. I'll be feelig better sood." I coughed a little more.

"Well, at least let me make you a cup of

herbal tea. It's good for your throat," said Mom. She stood up and headed for the stove.

"Thanks." I reached for the newspaper. Just then, I heard a roar from outside. "Oh, do!" I moaned.

"He's at it again," said Anna, craning her neck to peer out the kitchen window.

"I don't believe it," muttered my mom. She was at the sink now, filling the teakettle with water as she glared out the window. "Why can't he do that just a little bit later? Doesn't he realize that some people might still be trying to sleep?" She banged the kettle down on the stove and snapped on a burner.

The roar continued. It was Mr. Finch, our backyard neighbor, mowing his lawn. I didn't like the noise, but even more, I dreaded the newly cut grass. It never fails to make my allergies worse.

"Maybe I should talk to him," murmured Mom. "Ask him to wait until at least nine. Especially on weekends. I mean, eight is too early on a Monday, but remember last Saturday, when he started at seven-thirty?" She stood by the window, watching.

I didn't even look. I could picture the scene. Mr. Finch was a fastidious home owner, and he mowed his lawn at least twice a week, always early in the morning. He also clipped every stray blade of grass and weeded the walkways

4

until the yard looked ready for a military inspection. He didn't have any flower beds, but I imagined that if he did, the tulips would be lined up in straight rows and the roses would be pruned to within an inch of their lives.

Mr. Finch had moved into his house at about the same time we'd moved into ours. He didn't appear to have any family living with him, nor did we ever see friends stop by to visit. Mr. Finch was not a particularly neighborly neighbor; I couldn't imagine him dropping over for a cup of coffee or inviting us to a spontaneous backyard barbecue. No, Mr. Finch kept to himself, and I wasn't sorry. He didn't seem like a very friendly person.

"Don't bother talking to him, Mom," Anna advised. "I have a feeling Mr. Finch doesn't care if the noise bugs us. And after all, he has to listen to me practice for hours every afternoon."

"That's different," said my mother. "Your violin is hardly as noisy as his lawn mower, and the way you play, even scales sound delightful." She turned away from the window to bring me a steaming mug of tea. "Still, you're probably right. I have better things to do with my time. Speaking of which," she continued, glancing at her watch, "I have a train to catch." She picked up her cup for one last gulp of coffee, then put it down and grabbed her briefcase. "See you two around eight," she said, giving us each a quick hug. "Try to take it easy today," she told me seriously. "No racing around."

"Dod't worry," I said glumly. I felt too tired and dragged out to even think about taking my usual five-mile run after school. That was pretty amazing, since I don't usually let anything stand in the way of exercise. Trying to put on a brighter face to keep my mom from worrying, I took a sip of tea. "That's good," I said. "I feel better already."

My mother smiled. "I hope you'll feel a *lot* better by tonight." She stroked my hair. Then she was gone.

Anna and I finished up breakfast and put our dishes in the sink, all without talking much. The roar of Mr. Finch's mower filled the air, and I didn't feel like shouting over it. I don't think she did either.

I can often tell what Anna's feeling. As twins, we have a special bond. There have even been times when I've had a sudden twinge, a definite sensation that something was wrong with Anna — only to find out later that she'd fallen off her bike or had a fight with a friend. The same has happened to her. And when we were little, we were so close that we had a special made-up language all our own. Nobody else could understand, but the words made perfect sense to us.

Not long ago, a doctor discovered that we both have scoliosis, which is a curvature of the spine. Mine is very slight, but Anna's needs treatment. At first I felt so awful for her that I almost smothered her with caring and worry. These days, she treats her scoliosis the way I treat my asthma and allergies: as a minor inconvenience that barely slows her down and definitely doesn't keep her from enjoying life. She's still wearing a brace, but she's used to it and so am I.

One thing we're not completely used to, and probably never will be, is the fact that we don't have a dad anymore. Our father was killed in a car wreck about four years ago, and his absence has left a gaping hole in our lives. It's pretty hard to come to terms with such a huge, sudden loss, and I don't think any of us — Mom, Anna, or I — has completely worked through our feelings.

All I know is that I still miss my dad, every single day. I miss telling him about stuff, like the two incredible goals I made in a soccer game or about how I trimmed three seconds off my personal-best time for the hundred-yard dash. I hated that he wasn't around to see Anna and me become Bat Mitzvahs (we're

Jewish, and a Bat Mitzvah is a celebration of a young woman's entry into adulthood), and I miss his dumb jokes and his warm hugs and his harmonica playing and his everything.

But I also know that he's part of me — of us — now. I've taken to telling dumb jokes. Anna's learned to play the harmonica. And my mom, not a very demonstrative person before, has been working on her hugging skills.

Not long ago we even started visiting his grave, something I couldn't face for a long time. It feels good, like a connection with him. One time I left an old pair of soccer cleats there, as a symbol of the way I was growing up and moving on.

"Thinking about Dad?" Anna's voice broke into my thoughts.

"How did you know?" I asked, turning to face her. By then, we were both nearly ready to leave for school. I was in the front hall, stuffing my math book into my backpack. Anna was pulling a music stand out of the closet.

She shrugged. "I just did," she said. "You had that look on your face."

I knew exactly what she meant, because she has the same look whenever she's thinking about our father. Looking at Anna is sometimes like looking in the mirror. I smiled at her. She reached out and patted my shoulder. Then we opened the door and stepped outside. Mr.

Finch had finally finished mowing his lawn. Even from our front door I could hear the *snick-snick* of his clippers as he trimmed stray blades of grass. The smell of freshly cut lawn hung heavy in the still morning air.

I sneezed three times in a row.

"Thirty-wud, thirty-two, thirty-three," I said, smiling weakly at Anna. "It's goig to be a wodderful day."

CHAPTER 2

It wasn't a wodderful day. It was a long, horrible slog of a day, and by the time the last bell rang at school, I was ready to sleep for a week. I felt completely and totally exhausted. It was an effort just to keep my eyes open on the bus ride home.

I didn't even have the energy to make myself a snack. I just did the Frankenstein walk (arms outstretched, eyes half shut) to the couch, collapsed onto it, and fell into a deep sleep. And if I hadn't woken myself up with a coughing fit, I probably could have snoozed the whole afternoon and night away right there on the couch. As it was, I woke up before either Anna or Mom arrived home, feeling as foggy as if I'd never napped. I yawned, stretched, and checked my watch. Then I sat up with a start.

It was almost five-fifteen! Any second now, a car would be honking out front: my ride to the BSC meeting, which would begin at five-thirty.

After one last lung-busting round of coughing, I stood up — a bit unsteadily — and ran a hand through my hair. I sneezed four times, blew my nose, and wiped my eyes. Then I rummaged around in my backpack and pulled out a little vial of allergy pills. I was due to take one, so I shook one out and popped it into my mouth, washing it down with a swig from the bike bottle I carry around.

"Okay, then," I said to myself. "Ready? Ready!" It wasn't much of a pep talk, but it was all I could manage. I was extremely tired, and I felt as spacey as a Martian.

Just then, I heard the car horn I'd expected, so I dashed out to join Kristy — that's Kristy Thomas, president of the BSC and my neighbor — in the backseat of her brother Charlie's car. I slammed the car door behind me and adjusted my seat belt as Charlie revved the engine. As soon as I was settled, he took off with a rattle and a roar. (His car is known as the Junk Bucket. I think that's a *nice* name for it.)

I turned toward Kristy and smiled.

She gave a horrified gasp. "Ugh! Why are your eyes so red? You look awful," she said.

"Why, thaks," I replied. Nobody ever said I can't take a compliment gracefully. "You look terrific, yourself." Kristy, who has brown hair and eyes and is on the short side, was dressed in her usual "uniform" of jeans and a T-shirt.

She shrugged off my remark. "Maybe you should have stayed home," she said. "You must be really sick."

"It's just allergies. I cad bake it through the meeting," I said. I hate to miss BSC meetings. The club has been one of the best things about moving to Stoneybrook.

"You know best," said Kristy, shrugging. I could tell she didn't really believe I did, though. Kristy always thinks *she* knows best.

The funny thing is that she often does.

Kristy is president of the BSC because the club was her idea. She was the one who realized how much parents would like being able to call one number (on Mondays, Wednesdays, and Fridays, from five-thirty until six — that's when we meet) and reach a whole group of responsible, experienced sitters. She was also the one who figured out that there should be a club record book for keeping track of our schedules and our clients' addresses, and a club notebook for keeping track of what's going on with our charges. She came up with the idea for Kid-Kits (boxes stuffed with markers, toys, and books that we sometimes bring to jobs on rainy days), *and* she was the one who realized it would be good for the club to have associate members, who don't come to meetings but who are on standby for busy times.

By now you're beginning to understand that Kristy is an idea person. This is true. She's also a good leader (some people call her bossy) and a smart businessperson. You see, the BSC is more like a business than a club, and Kristy functions as its CEO (Chief Executive Officer).

How did Kristy come to be the person she is? Well, I think it's because of her family life. For one thing, her mom's an incredibly strong role model. She brought up four kids (Kristy, her two older brothers, and a younger brother) on her own after Kristy's dad walked out on the family long ago.

For another thing, Kristy has had to learn to be organized, since her family is now so huge and complicated. It's no longer just Kristy and her mom and her brothers. Kristy's mom remarried. Her new husband is a terrific guy who happens to be a millionaire *and* who has two kids from an earlier marriage. After the wedding Kristy's mom and Watson, Kristy's new stepdad, adopted a toddler (a Vietnamese orphan). These days, their house is no less than chaotic at all times. Kristy's grandmother lives with the family too, and there are all kinds of pets (I can't keep count — all I know is that I'm allergic to most of them) running around. Fortunately, the house is huge, a mansion, actually.

I like Kristy, but sometimes I think we're almost too much alike ever to be true best friends. We're both stubborn and outspoken, and we're both pretty athletic and competitive. Kristy's favorite sport is softball, and I've been helping her coach this team she manages for very young kids. She's great with the kids, patient and kind.

"Abby, wake up!" Kristy was nudging my shoulder. Charlie had pulled up in front of Claudia Kishi's house, which is where the BSC meets. (Before she moved to Watson's mansion, Kristy lived across the street from Claudia.) "We're here."

"I wasd't sleepig," I insisted. "Just studyig the idside of by eyelids." That was one of my dad's old jokes.

Kristy rolled her eyes. "Whatever," she said. "Let's go."

We let ourselves into the house and thumped up the stairs to Claudia's room. (Well, Kristy thumped. I dragged.) Claudia welcomed us, but I barely even said hello. I just did the Frankenstein thing again, heading straight for her bed. I lay down across it and shut my eyes — just for a second.

The jangling of a phone woke me up. For a moment, I had no idea where I was or what time it was or even *who* I was. I tried to jump up to answer the phone, but my body wouldn't obey. Fortunately, someone else picked it up.

"Sure, Mrs. Rodowsky. Wednesday afternoon will be no problem. We'll call you back to let you know who's taking the job."

That was Claudia talking. Slowly, it all came back to me. I was at a BSC meeting, and as I looked around the room I realized that all the other members had arrived. Not only that, but Kristy must have already called the meeting to order, because a glance at the clock told me it was 5:35.

Claudia turned to Mary Anne Spier, the club secretary. "Who's free on Wednesday?" she asked. I noticed that Claudia and Mary Anne were both sitting on the floor — probably because I was hogging the bed, where they usually sit. Oops.

But Claudia didn't look uncomfortable. She was reclining on this cool oversize pillow she'd covered in fake leopard skin and trimmed with gold braid. She looked exotic and artistic and relaxed as she unwrapped the foil from a Hershey's Kiss while she waited for Mary Anne to answer.

Claudia is way cool, no doubt about it. She's also, artistically speaking, the most talented person I've ever met. Not only does she draw and paint really well, but she makes her own jewelry, customizes her clothes, and creates hairstyles that make your jaw drop.

Claudia is Japanese-American, with long black hair and beautiful dark almond-shaped eyes. She lives with her mom and dad and an older sister who is basically a genius. Claud's grandmother Mimi used to live with the family, but she died before I moved here. I wish I could have met her. She sounds like the warmest, most accepting person in the world, and I know she was very important to Claudia. Mimi was supportive of everything Claudia did and never cared that she doesn't do well in school (Claud even had to spend some time repeating seventh grade recently), or that she would live on junk food if she could, and would read nothing but Nancy Drew books. (Mr. and Mrs. Kishi do care about all of the above, so Claudia works hard to try to pull decent grades and is careful to hide her Milk Duds and her mysteries.)

As vice-president of the BSC, Claudia's official duties include — well, not much. Unofficially, she's responsible for providing munchies for our meetings. However, we do meet in her room because she's the only member with her own phone and phone number, which are essential for our business.

Meanwhile, back at the meeting . . . it took

Mary Anne just seconds to check the record book and learn that Kristy and I were the only ones free to sit for the three Rodowsky boys.

"I can take it," said Kristy, reaching for the phone to call Mrs. Rodowsky back. (See how well the BSC system works?) "I don't think Abby's in any shape to deal with the Walking Disaster." (That's our private nickname for Jackie Rodowsky, who is a wonderful but incredibly accident-prone little boy.)

At that, all eyes turned to me. Mary Anne's were full of concern. "Are you okay, Abby?" she asked. Mary Anne is by far the most caring, sensitive member of our club.

"I'll be fide," I said hoarsely. "It's just by allergies kickig id, big-tibe."

"Can we do anything to help?" she asked.

"Short of vacuubig all the polled out of the atbosphere, probably dot," I joked. My laugh turned into a cough, but I recovered quickly. "Thaks adyway. Add Kristy's right. I guess I do't feel up to sittig for the Rodowskys."

Mary Anne smiled at me. "I don't blame you," she said. "They can be a handful." She made a note about the job in the club record book.

Mary Anne, who looks a little like Kristy with her brown eyes and hair, is an excellent secretary. She's neat and thorough, and I hear she's never once made a mistake in scheduling.

Her dad's a neat freak too. And he used to be very strict, but that was before I knew Mary Anne, so it's hard to imagine. Mary Anne's mom died back when Mary Anne was just a baby. I can relate to how it feels to be a kid in a one-parent family. It must have been even harder for Mary Anne, since she was an only child.

These days Mr. Spier seems pretty easygoing. Maybe it's because he's married again, to a woman who was his high school sweetheart long ago. She'd moved away to California, married, and had two kids, Dawn and Jeff. When her marriage broke up, she and the kids came back to Stoneybrook. Mary Anne became best friends with Dawn Schafer, and soon afterward Mary Anne's dad and Dawn's mom fell in love again. Suddenly, Mary Anne's family had grown a lot larger.

But Jeff never adjusted to living in Stoneybrook, and he went back to California to live with his dad. Eventually, Dawn did the same. Poor Mary Anne lost a stepsister and a best friend. Fortunately, she still has another best friend (Kristy — talk about opposites attracting!), a kitten named Tigger, and a boyfriend named Logan Bruno. (Logan's one of those associate members I mentioned earlier. The other is a girl named Shannon Kilbourne, who lives in Kristy's and my neighborhood.)

18

Dawn is now an honorary member of the BSC. She used to be the alternate officer, which meant that she could fill in for any other officer who couldn't come to a meeting. Guess who holds that job now? Correctamundo. It's *moi*. And all I can say is that it was a good thing everybody was at the meeting that day. I mean, what if I'd actually had to *do* something at it?

For instance, Stacey has a big job. That's Stacey McGill, the club treasurer and Claudia's best friend. Toward the end of the meeting, just as I was drifting off for another little nap, I heard Kristy ask if there was any other business.

"You know there is," Stacey said teasingly. "Come on, everybody, cough it up." She held out a manila envelope: the club's treasury. Stacey is responsible for collecting dues each Monday and for keeping track of the club finances. We use the dues to pay Claudia's phone bill and to help buy gas for the Junk Bucket, and for the occasional pizza party, when Stacey says we have enough to spare.

Everybody groaned and reached into pockets and backpacks. We always give Stacey a hard time, but nobody really minds paying dues.

Stacey passed the envelope around. "There's almost enough in there for this adorable leather jacket I saw at the mall yesterday," she said.

"You guys wouldn't mind if I did a little embezzling, would you?"

We cracked up. Stacey would never run off with the club's money. But if she did, I can just imagine her heading straight to Washington Mall. Stacey lives for fashion. She grew up as an only child in Manhattan, which is Fashion Central. Now that her parents are divorced, she lives with her mom in Stoneybrook but visits her dad often. He still lives in the land of Bloomingdale's and Barney's.

Stacey's sophisticated, polished, and very pretty, with beautiful blue eyes and a curly mane of blonde hair. I admire her for the way she's handled her parents' divorce, and for the way she deals with being diabetic. Do you know anyone with diabetes? In case you don't, I'll explain. Diabetes is a lifelong disease that affects the way the body processes sugar. The pancreas produces a hormone called insulin, which helps the body use the fuel it's given (food, in other words). When someone has diabetes the pancreas doesn't work right. That can't be fixed, but diabetes can be managed. Stacey keeps hers under control by being very, very careful about what she eats. She also has to give herself injections of insulin every day, which can't be fun.

The treasury envelope was passed from hand to hand around the room until it found its way to Mallory Pike and Jessica Ramsey, the BSC's junior officers, who were sitting in their usual spots on the floor. Mal and Jessi are eleven and in the sixth grade, instead of thirteen and in the eighth, like the rest of us. They're only allowed to take afternoon jobs (unless they're sitting for their own siblings), but they're both good, responsible sitters.

"If my brothers and sisters had a chance to embezzle some funds they'd be heading straight for the hardware store," Mal commented. "They're completely caught up in that go-cart competition. It's all they can think about. They're spending their life savings on parts."

I was really excited about the go-cart competition. The Stoneybrook Community Center was sponsoring it as a special fund-raiser, and it was going to take place soon. Teams of kids were building their own go-carts for the race. The winners could designate which charity their prize money would go to. I thought the project sounded cool.

Mal's younger siblings could make up a team and pit crew all by themselves: There are seven of them! That's one reason she's such a good sitter.

Mal has pale skin and reddish-brown hair, and wears glasses and braces (she hates both with a passion). She loves to read and write, and she wants to be a children's book author and illustrator someday.

Jessi, her best friend, has cocoa-brown skin, dark eyes, and a lean, strong body just made for dancing. She's a serious student of ballet and practices as hard as any athlete. Jessi has a younger sister and a baby brother, and lives with her parents and an aunt.

"Becca's talking about building a go-cart too," she said. "She and Charlotte Johanssen are talking about putting together an all-girl team."

"Cool!" I said. "Do they deed a coach? I'd love to help." Just then, I was struck by another coughing fit. It took me a few moments to recover. "As sood as I'b well, that is," I added when I could speak again.

"Abby, you're not going to get well unless you take care of yourself," said Mary Anne. "I think you need to go right home and rest."

"I second the motion," said Kristy. "And I'll even provide the ride home, since this meeting is hereby declared over."

"Thaks," I said weakly. Suddenly, I couldn't wait to be in my own bed. It had occurred to me that what I was dealing with might be something more than just my familiar old allergies.

CHAPTER 3

"Loocy, I tol' you, you can't be in the show —"

Click.

"The young spotted salamander holds his ground as the toad attacks fearlessly, inching forward —"

Click.

"Oh, José, I never knew love could be like this — or perhaps I did, before I was kidnapped and developed amnesia —"

Click.

"That's right, Mrs. Spooner. By picking door number three, you've won a brand-new —"

Click.

I hit the mute button and groaned. I'd been watching TV for four solid hours, and I felt as if I'd seen everything at least twice. Dumb videos on MTV. *I Love Lucy* reruns I knew by heart. Game shows. Nature shows. Soap operas. Talk shows about stuff I'd never heard of and never wanted to hear about again.

On the screen, a slick-looking guy with a microphone let a skinny woman in a frilly dress hug him as she screamed with joy. (Fortunately, that mute button I'd hit silenced her screams.) Then he led her to her prize, a washer-dryer set. She stroked the appliances, acting as if all her dreams had come true.

I couldn't relate.

But the way I was feeling, I couldn't relate to much of anything. It was the day after our BSC meeting, and I'd woken up feeling sicker than ever. For some reason, my nose wasn't quite so stuffed up, but everything hurt, including breathing. I could barely move.

"Ma?" I'd called that morning when I heard my mother bustling about down the hall.

She came into my room. "What is it, honey?" she asked as she tucked in her blouse.

"I don't feel so good."

She took a closer look at me. "I bet you don't," she said. "You look like something the cat dragged in."

"We don't have a cat. I'm allergic to kitty litter, remember?"

"It's just a saying," she murmured absently as she put her hand on my forehead. "Mmm, you feel like you're burning up. Let's take your temperature." She ran to the bathroom and came back with the thermometer, which she stuck under my tongue.

"Is your throat sore?" she asked me.

"Mmuugggg," I said, trying to talk around the thermometer. (I was trying to say "majorly.") In fact, my throat felt as if it were on fire.

"And I heard you coughing once during the night," she said. "But when I checked on you, you seemed to be sleeping, so I didn't wake you."

As far as I could remember, I'd tossed and turned and hadn't slept a wink all night.

"What's wrong with Abby?" asked Anna, coming into my room.

"She's not feeling well," said my mom. "And it could be contagious, so you're probably better off staying away from her for now." She removed the thermometer and checked it. "Mmm-hmm," she said. "You do have a fever. You're going to have to stay home from school today."

"Bummer," I said as cheerfully as my sore throat would allow. "Guess I'll have to lounge around all day and eat bonbons. What a shame." A day off didn't sound so bad, but I'd have liked to be feeling better so I could really enjoy it.

So there I was, Miss Couch Potato of the Year, all settled in on the living room sofa, surrounded by pillows, covered by a light quilt, with bottles of ginger ale and water within easy reach. The TV remote and the Kleenex box were both nearby, and Mom had left me about a week's supply of fruit.

"If you can, try to heat up some soup for yourself at noontime," she said. I could tell she felt guilty about heading off to work while I was at death's door.

"I — I don't think I'll have the energy," I said, draping a hand across my forehead in an imitation of an old-time movie heroine.

"Oh, *you*," she said, giving me a wry smile.

I smiled back. I could remember my dad when he had a cold. He'd play it for all it was worth and end up being waited on hand and foot by the rest of us.

Anna had loaned me her favorite Mozart CD. "These piano sonatas always make me feel better," she explained. And she promised to skip orchestra rehearsal and come straight home after school to check on how I was doing.

If I still had a fever by the time my mom came home, we were going to call Dr. Hernandez. I hoped we wouldn't have to, but on the other hand I did want to feel better soon. I didn't really mind missing school, but I hated to miss too many days of exercise. Being fit is important to me.

But that afternoon, running seemed like

something I'd done in another life. I was still recovering after my last journey from the couch to the bathroom and back. I couldn't imagine having enough energy to run around the block, much less five miles.

I sighed, pulled the quilt up around my chin, and zapped the TV remote, turning the volume back on.

"— and today's lucky grand-prize winner will be receiving —"

Click.

"We want to be your long-distance company —"

Click.

"I love you, you love me, we're a —"

Click-click-click-click.

I held the button down and let the images fly by. Soon I'd be bored enough to put on that CD Anna had lent me. Then something caught my eye. The opening credits — in blood red — of a show called *Mystery Trackers*.

I'd heard kids talking about it at school, but I'd never seen it myself. Here was my big chance. I turned up the volume a notch or two and listened.

Loud, insistent music played as black-and-white mug shots of nasty-looking criminals filled the screen in quick succession, "WANTED" stamped across their faces in red. Over the music, a man's voice intoned, "Welcome to *Mys-*

tery Trackers, the show that lets you be the detective."

I listened closer, already forgetting my boredom. I love mysteries — everyone in the BSC does — and I've even helped solve a few.

"Today you'll meet three criminals who are wanted by state and federal officials. Wanted, but not captured. That's where you come in. These people may live in your community, shop in your grocery store, relax in your parks. We need your help to find them and bring them to justice."

I nodded. "Okay," I said to the screen. "So, what do I do?"

"If you spot one of the criminals you'll meet on this show," the announcer said as if answering my question, "do not — I repeat, *do not* — attempt to apprehend the person yourself. Your safety comes first. Instead, contact your local law enforcement agency or call this number."

He reeled off an 800 number, the same one that now appeared in yellow type across the bottom of the screen. Then the show switched to a commercial.

I sat up to pour myself a glass of ginger ale. Then I plumped up my pillows, shook out my quilt, and made myself comfortable. This was one show I could stick with. I had a feeling I would enjoy it.

Sure enough, I did. Learning about these criminals was fascinating. What had made them go wrong? Why did they feel they were above the law? Did they really imagine they'd get away with their crimes?

The first one was a bank robber. The announcer told the story of his career, starting with small heists and moving up to major moolah. The guy was not a particularly talented thief. He was a bumbler and came close to being caught every time. But somehow he was lucky — or, to put it better, the police were unlucky. Even though his picture and description were posted in banks across the country, the criminal had stayed out of their clutches.

The second was a woman, which surprised me, though I don't know why. I guess women can commit crimes just as easily as men. Anyway, she'd held up a small-town post office, which didn't make her very popular with the federal government. She was small and dark-haired and looked as if she could fit in just about anywhere.

The third was a man who'd messed up a lot of people's lives. First, he embezzled from the company he worked for, driving it into bankruptcy. Then he'd abandoned his family after stealing his wife's life savings. Nice guy, huh?

The show held my interest to the end. But it was followed by a dumb program about aliens landing somewhere out West, and I ended up channel surfing for another half hour until I fell asleep, holding the remote.

When Anna came home and woke me up, I told her all about *Mystery Trackers*. I could tell she thought it was trash, but she listened to me patiently, I guess because I was sick and she was trying to be nice.

"The funny thing," I told her when I'd finished describing the show, "is that I thought one of the people looked familiar. I just can't remember which one. . . ." I really couldn't. My mind was pretty foggy at that point.

Anna laid a cool hand on my forehead. "That's okay," she said, humoring me. "You know, I think you do still have a fever. Let's take your temperature. Remember, Mom said she wanted to take you to see Dr. Hernandez if you still had a fever this afternoon."

Anna went to find the thermometer, and I lay back on the couch, exhausted again. She was probably right to think I was being silly. After all, I bet everyone who watches those shows thinks the criminals look familiar. If you watched it daily, you'd probably start seeing criminals around every corner. The people staffing that 800 number must receive hundreds of panicked phone calls every day. *Well*, I decided, as Anna returned with the thermometer, *this is one Mystery Tracker who's not going to let her imagination run away with her*. Even in the grip of a fever (Anna turned out to be right), I was too smart to let that happen.

CHAPTER 4

Have you ever experienced true boredom? I mean, boredom beyond belief? Have you ever been so bored that the idea of sitting through a class with your most unexciting teacher droning on and on begins to sound like the most fascinating thing imaginable?

If so, you *still* don't know how bored I was by Wednesday, because my boredom was even more excruciating than that. I was bored stiff. Bored to tears. Bored to death.

It was only my second day home from school, but I was about to lose my mind. I couldn't even turn on the TV anymore — that's how sick of it I was. I'd read until my eyes were about to drop out of my head, and I'd written letters to every pen pal I'd had since the age of six, and I'd even picked thousands of those little pill-y things off my favorite pair of soccer socks.

I was still feeling sick, but not sick enough to

sleep the hours away. Mom had come home from work early in order to hustle me to Dr. Hernandez on Tuesday night, and he'd informed us that what I had was bronchitis. "It won't go away overnight either," he'd cautioned. "Your allergies are a complication."

The good news was that he'd given me some medicine and told me that I'd stop being contagious after I'd been on it for twenty-four hours. I'd have to stay home from school for at least the rest of the week, and probably for most of the next week too. If I didn't take care of myself, he warned me, I could develop pneumonia and have to be hospitalized.

There had been moments already when I'd wondered if that wouldn't be more fun — or at least more interesting — than lying around at home.

"I envy you," Anna had said. "If I had all that free time, I'd finally be able to finish reading that biography of Beethoven. And I could catalog my CD collection and work on my composition for my Advanced Music Theory class."

I won't tell you what I said to that, since it wasn't very nice.

In case you haven't noticed, I do not cope well with being sick. While some people (Anna, for example) might welcome a break in their routine, I am not one of them. I need to be in constant motion. Sitting still for any length of time makes me nuts.

Anyway, it was Wednesday afternoon. I'd already eaten my lunch (chicken noodle soup and some crackers, plus a nectarine) and finished the homework Anna had brought home for me the night before (thanks a lot, sis!). I'd watched enough TV to feel brainwashed (ever catch yourself singing a diaper commercial jingle while you're doing the dishes?), and I wasn't sleepy enough to take a nap.

I looked out the window, hoping for inspiration. I was in my room, which has two windows. The one I was looking out faces Kristy's house. I could just see it when I peered past Mrs. Porter's, which sits between our houses. The other window faces toward the backyard, and I usually keep that shade pulled down, so the sun doesn't wake me up too early.

The window that looks toward Kristy's has a built-in window seat, comfy cushions on top and a bookshelf below. I can curl up on the seat and read by the light of the window — when I'm in a reading kind of mood, that is. That day I wasn't. I was in a tearing-my-hair-out-with-boredom kind of mood.

There's a big maple tree in our front yard, and a couple of its branches reach toward my window. I like looking out at the green and imagining what it would be like to be a squirrel, with a huge tree like that for my playground. I didn't see any squirrels that day, but I did see something else.

It was a flash of color — red, to be exact. With some black and white below. A bird clinging to the trunk of the tree. "Cool," I said out loud. "Looks like that woodpecker is back." A woodpecker had been hanging around all winter, and as a treat for it, Anna had put out suet (gross stuff that birds love — it's like a big hunk of fat). But a couple of months ago, the woodpecker had disappeared. Anna would be happy to hear that it had returned.

I hopped down off the window seat and headed into Anna's room to find the binoculars. They used to be Dad's, but now we all use them. Anna's the one who does the most bird-watching, though. Probably because she has the most patience for it.

Binoculars in hand, I settled back on the window seat and began to scan the tree. Within a couple of moments I'd brought the woodpecker into my sights. He was a cool-looking bird, all right, with his black and white stripes and bright red head.

But you know what? He was kind of boring. All he was doing was walking up and down the trunk of the tree, stopping occasionally to drill his yellow beak into the bark, looking for insects to eat. One of those nature shows could probably make a whole hour of it, but I was yawning after thirty seconds.

I was just about to put the binoculars down when something bright yellow caught my eye. Something yellow and *huge*. For a moment, I was confused. Then I lowered the binoculars and realized that I was staring at a school bus. I checked my watch. Sure enough, school was over.

The bus stopped at the corner, and a few kids jumped out. A few minutes later, another bus pulled over. Kids were arriving home from Stoneybrook Elementary, Stoneybrook Academy, and Stoneybrook Day School. I lifted the binoculars again and watched. I saw Karen Brewer jump off her bus, looking a bit lonely. She's Kristy's stepsister, and she's in second grade at Stoneybrook Academy. I think she misses her younger brother, Andrew, who's living in Chicago now for a few months, with his mom and stepdad.

Next, I saw Druscilla Porter. Druscilla is the same age as Karen. She headed straight to her grandmother's house (her grandmother is Mrs. Porter, my next-door neighbor), looking glum. Druscilla is not the happiest child in the world. Her parents are in the midst of a nasty divorce, and it hasn't been easy for her.

I trained the binoculars on Karen again and watched her watch Druscilla go inside. I figured Karen was thinking about what it would be like to live with Morbidda Destiny, which is what she calls Mrs. Porter. Karen has a very active imagination, and she's decided, for various reasons, that our elderly neighbor is a witch.

I spotted the Hsu brothers too, Timmy and Scott, who live down the block. They're members of Kristy's Krushers, the softball team I co-manage. With the binoculars I could see that Timmy had a skinned knee. Maybe he'd gotten that by sliding into second base at a recent practice I'd missed. Scott was wearing Hercules underwear (the waistband was poking out from the top of his jeans).

I also saw Shannon Kilbourne's little sisters, Tiffany and Maria, who go to Stoneybrook Day, as well as the Papadakis kids, Hannie and Linny, who have a preschool-age sister named Sari. They live next door to the Kilbournes, across the street from Kristy. Then I spotted the older Korman kids, Bill and Melody (they have a baby sister named Skylar), who live across from me. It was fun to check out what they were wearing, what kind of moods they seemed to be in, and what books they'd brought home from school. If I worked at it, maybe I could learn to lip-read, so I could "eavesdrop" on their conversations.

I was starting to enjoy this. Why hadn't I thought of watching my neighbors with binoculars before? (I didn't want to call it spying. That made it sound wrong somehow. I was just . . . looking.)

A sputtering, clanking sound made me swing the binoculars around until I saw the Junk Bucket come into view down the street. Charlie was at the wheel, and a very pretty red-haired girl sat next to him in the passenger seat. Did Charlie have a new girlfriend? I was going to have to ask Kristy about that. He pulled into their driveway and hopped out, but the girl waited in the car. Charlie was probably just running inside for something. At that moment, a jet roared by overhead, and Charlie glanced up to see it. I jerked back from the window, afraid he might see me and think I was snooping.

Me? Snooping? Never!

Kristy came home moments later. I knew she'd been dropped off at the corner by our school bus, which I like to call the Wheeze Wagon because of the way it chugs up hills, sounding as if it's on its last legs. She ran inside without a glance around and soon after came back out, munching on an apple (a green Granny Smith, to be exact). Charlie was right behind her, and they both jumped into the Junk Bucket and took off. Suddenly I remembered.

Kristy had a job with the Rodowskys, and Charlie must be driving her there.

After the last sputters of the Junk Bucket faded away, activity in the neighborhood seemed to grind to a halt. I swept the binoculars back and forth but didn't catch sight of any movement.

Then I heard a familiar sound from the backyard. *Snick, snick. Snick, snick.* Was Mr. Finch trimming his grass again already?

I moved to the other window and raised the shade. That window has no window seat, so I pulled my desk chair over in order to be comfortable. Then I raised the binoculars and looked.

The *snicking* sound wasn't coming from Mr. Finch's house, after all. It was Ms. Fielding, our other backyard neighbor. She was out there in her big straw hat, pruning her prize rosebushes, the ones she fusses over all summer long. She feeds them and waters them and picks bugs off them and, if you ever start a conversation with her, talks your ear off about them.

I swung the binoculars around, checking Mr. Finch's backyard, just for kicks. I was a little surprised to see him lying in a lounge chair, relaxing. It seemed early for him to be home from work, but for all I knew he was always home that early. I'd never even glanced at his yard in the afternoon before. I was a little annoyed too. Why couldn't he be mowing his lawn now, instead of at the crack of dawn?

Maybe he was sick, like me. I focused the binoculars on his face to get a better look at him.

And that's when it hit me.

That criminal I'd seen on *Mystery Trackers*? The one who looked familiar?

He was the spitting image of Mr. Finch.

But that was ridiculous.

Wasn't it?

CHAPTER 5

Wednesday

Funny. We thought this go-cart project would be all about cooperation and good times. I suppose we should have known better.

It'll be fun in the end, I'm sure. Won't it?

I bet it will. But try telling Nicky that.

Poor Nicky.

"Aww, poor Nicky."

"I know. I wish there was something we could do. But we can't exactly *make* the triplets let him on their team."

While I was keeping an eye on my neighbors, Mal and Stacey were sitting in lawn chairs in the Pikes' driveway, keeping an eye on the proceedings in the garage.

Mal was watching some of her brothers and sisters while Mrs. Pike did some work inside. Stacey was sitting for Charlotte Johanssen, who happens to be one of her favorite charges. (Charlotte's eight and an only child. She and Stacey are so close that they call each other "almost sisters.") That afternoon, Charlotte's dad had driven Charlotte, Becca Ramsey (Jessi's sister), and Stacey to the Pikes', since they were planning to work on their go-cart with Vanessa, Mal's nine-year-old sister. They were pretty excited about their all-girl team. Meanwhile, the Pike triplets had formed a team of their own.

The Pikes' garage was overflowing with kids, tools, and go-cart parts, all in an incredible jumble.

"Have you seen that wrench I was using?" Adam yelled to his brothers. Jordan and Byron were only three feet away, doing something with a screwdriver and a hammer, so Adam didn't really have to yell. But the triplets are like that. They're ten, and if you know ten-year-old boys, you know there's nothing they like better than to be noisy.

"Is this it?" Nicky Pike, who's eight, picked up a tool and held it out to Adam.

Adam scowled. "I thought we told you to stay out of here."

"You can't make me," said Nicky. "It's my garage as much as yours."

Adam was still scowling. "Well, we don't need your help, anyway. Our team is full. Go find another team to join."

Nicky shrugged. Stacey and Mal were watching and could tell that he was upset. But he didn't say anything. He just set the wrench back on the shelf where he'd found it and walked away. As soon as his back was turned, Adam picked up the wrench.

Mal scowled. "Poor Nicky," she said. "All he wants is to feel as if he's a part of things." It's an old story. The triplets are always teasing Nicky and leaving him out.

Mal and Stacey watched as Nicky ambled over to where Vanessa, Charlotte, and Becca were examining an old washtub. "This could work," Becca was saying excitedly. "I mean, it may not look super-cool, but it makes a good place for the driver to sit in. If we can figure out how to attach wheels . . ."

"I have an idea," Nicky offered.

Vanessa turned to look at him. "Scram, scat, get out of town! We don't need any boys around!"

Have I mentioned that Vanessa wants to be a poet someday? She often talks in verse. But this was one poem that didn't go over well with its audience. Mal told me later that she saw Nicky's eyes fill with tears.

"Maybe Claire and Margo would like to be on a team with you," she suggested to Nicky. Claire is the youngest Pike, at five. Margo's seven.

Nicky just rolled his eyes. "Right," he said. "Sure. Like they'd be any help at all." He shook his head. "Anyway, they don't want to build a go-cart. They just want to watch the races. That's why they're not around today."

Margo and Claire were off playing with friends. And Mal knew Nicky was right. Neither of the girls was interested in building a go-cart.

"I bet you'll find a team to join," said Stacey. "Meanwhile, why don't you hang out with us? You know we love your company."

Nicky blushed. Mal could tell he was flattered. "Okay," he said. He pulled up a lawn chair. "Want to hear my idea for the fastest go-cart in the world?"

With Stacey and Mal as a captive audience, Nicky forgot his troubles for the moment and rambled on and on. Meanwhile, construction — and arguments — continued as the other kids worked on their go-carts.

"What about using these bicycle handlebars for steering?" Jordan asked, holding up a rusted piece of metal.

"That must be one of the parts from our first tricycles," said Adam, laughing. "Remember when we took them apart? Dad was so mad!"

"But then he said it must mean we were ready for grown-up bikes," said Jordan.

"And we refused to have training wheels," Byron said. He was laughing too.

Mal was trying to pay attention to Nicky, but she heard the triplets. She couldn't help cracking up as she remembered that time. Her mother kept complaining that she couldn't seem to keep enough Band-Aids on hand to keep up with the cuts and scrapes. Mr. Pike said he wished he had stock in the company.

Meanwhile, Jordan was digging through the pile of parts he'd come across. "Look," he said. "There're lots of wheels in here too. And pedals. I wonder if we're allowed to have pedals."

"They didn't say anything about pedals," said Adam. "I saw the flier. It just said the go-carts couldn't be motorized."

So much for Nicky's plans, which involved rocket fuel. Mal figured that just might fall into the "motorized" category.

"I think the go-carts are just supposed to roll down the hill," Stacey said. "Like a soapbox derby. So probably pedals would be out."

"Okay," said Jordan, tossing the pedals over his shoulder.

In another corner of the garage, Vanessa, Becca, and Charlotte were taking a short candy break. Suddenly, Becca let out a loud whoop.

"What is it? What is it?" asked Mal. "Are you okay? Do you need the Heimlich maneuver?" (We've all learned how to save someone who's choking. It's a good thing for any baby-sitter — or any person, for that matter — to know how to do.)

"No, no, I'm fine," said Becca, who was up on her feet and dancing around. "But look! We're *definitely* going to win this race."

She was waving a little square of red paper.

"What's that?" asked Stacey.

"It's the wrapper from a Tootsie Roll Pop," said Becca, as if that explained everything.

"And?" prompted Mal.

"It has an Indian on it," said Becca. "I mean, a Native American. The one who's shooting an arrow at a star."

"I still don't understand," said Stacey.

"It means good luck!" said Charlotte. "Everybody knows that."

"The cowboy on the wrapper is good luck too," added Vanessa. Then she started chanting: "The news is in! We're going to win!"

The other girls picked it up, and the three of them marched around, repeating the chant.

The triplets ignored them. "You know what we need?" asked Adam, who'd been deep in thought. "A really good name for our team."

"Definitely," said Byron.

The boys put aside their tools and sat down to discuss the matter.

"How about The Terrible Three?" Byron asked.

"I don't know," said Adam. "It should be something that shows how fast we are, like The Pike Express."

Jordan wrinkled his nose. "The Pike Express?" he repeated. "Uh-uh. That sounds like a train."

"Do you have a better idea?" asked Adam.

"Let me think," said Jordan. He frowned at the girls, who were still marching around chanting, and put his hands over his ears. "I know, I know!" he said, after he'd thought for a moment. "How about The Speedy Three?"

Adam nodded. So did Byron.

"Excellent," said Adam.

"Awesome," said Byron.

The boys gave each other high fives. Then they started sorting through parts again.

Meanwhile, the girls had decided that their team also needed a name.

"What about Wild Women?" asked Becca.

Charlotte giggled. "We're not women yet," she said. "How about Glory Girls?"

"I like it, I like it," said Vanessa. "All those in favor?"

Each of the girls raised a hand.

"It's unanimous!" cried Becca. "Go, Glory Girls!"

"Go, Glory Girls!" echoed Vanessa and Charlotte. The triplets watched and shook their heads. And Mal and Stacey just smiled at each other.

So far, an entire afternoon had passed without much actual work being done on the go-carts. But the squabbling had stopped and the kids were having fun. Now, if only Nicky could find a team that would take him in . . .

CHAPTER 6

"I hereby call this meeting to order!"

Those words were music to my ears. It felt so incredibly good to be out of my house, to be with friends, to be at a BSC meeting.

Even though I was still feeling pretty awful by Wednesday afternoon, I'd called my mother at work and begged her to let me go to the meeting. "It's been almost twenty-four hours, so I'm not contagious anymore," I'd pointed out. "And I think it would do me good to go out. I'll only be out of bed for an hour or so — what harm could it do?"

Reluctantly, she'd agreed. "But take it slow," she'd said, "and I want you to come straight home afterward."

I'd promised I would.

What I didn't tell my mother was this: It wasn't just that I wanted to go to the meeting for fun. No, there was more to it than that. I had an agenda. I needed my friends to help me catch a crook.

First, though, I had to wait my turn. I tried to be patient while Stacey and Mal talked about the go-cart teams. I listened to everything Kristy had to say about her job with the Rodowsky boys. And I thanked Claudia for the Ring-Dings she was passing around.

But it was hard to wait — oh, man, it was hard to wait.

Finally, the moment arrived.

"Any new business?" Kristy asked.

My hand shot up. "I have some!" I cried.

Everybody looked at me.

"You have new business?" asked Kristy. "But you've been home for the last two days."

"I know," I said. "Believe me, I know. But here's the thing: I think we have a mystery on our hands!"

At that, everyone leaned forward, interested.

Unfortunately, the phone picked that moment to ring, and I had to wait another three minutes while Mary Anne arranged a sitter for a job at the Hobarts'.

The second she hung up, she turned to me. "Okay, tell us! What's going on?"

"Have any of you ever seen the movie *Rear Window*?" I asked, raising my eyebrows.

"What?" Kristy sounded as if she were about to blow her top. "I thought you were going to tell us about a mystery. Now you want to talk about movies?"

"You're kidding," Mary Anne said to me, ignoring her friend. "What did you see? A murder?" Her eyes grew round. She looked scared, but excited.

"What are you two talking about?" asked Mal.

The others were confused too. So Mary Anne — who's a classic-movie buff like me — and I had to stop to tell them the plot of one of the best Alfred Hitchcock movies.

"See, there's this photographer guy who has a broken leg," I began, "and he's stuck at home in his apartment."

"So he starts watching out the window, just for fun," Mary Anne added, "and he sees all this stuff that goes on in his neighborhood."

"Including —" I paused dramatically, "a murder."

"Well, he doesn't actually *see* the murder," put in Mary Anne. "That's what makes it a mystery. He just thinks that his neighbor killed his wife, based on some stuff he's seen."

"Like, the guy stuffing something into a trunk!" I interrupted gleefully.

"Ew!" cried Jessi and Mal.

"But nobody else believes him," Mary Anne continued.

"So, did it happen or not?" asked Kristy.

"For the answer to that, you're going to have to watch the movie," I said teasingly. "For now, the main thing you have to know is that the guy sees a crime — or thinks he does — while he's watching out his window."

"So you've been —" Stacey began.

"Spying on your neighbors?" Kristy finished, looking a little uncomfortable.

"No!" I said. "Not spying. Just watching a little. You know, like when I walk past the window or something." I thought of myself camped on the window seat with the binoculars and blushed. "Anyway, the point is that I think one of my neighbors might be a criminal!"

"Whoa!" said Claudia. "What do you mean?"

I told my friends about watching *Mystery Trackers*, and how I'd seen the profiles of three criminals. Then I told my friends how one of them had looked familiar, but how I couldn't put my finger on which one it had been. Finally, I told them about seeing Mr. Finch in his backyard. "It was him!" I said. "I'd swear by it."

"*Which* him?" asked Mary Anne. "The bank robber or the embezzler?"

"I don't know," I admitted. "You have to understand, I've kind of been in a fog for the last two days."

"A fog is right," said Kristy. "Mr. Finch, a criminal? Are you sure you don't still have a fever?" She laughed. "Mr. Finch is as normal as they come. You should see this guy," she told the rest of our friends. "All he does is mow his lawn. I mean, sure, he does it at weird times, but that hardly makes him a bank robber." She shook her head. "I think you've seen that *Back Window* movie one too many times."

"It's *REAR Window*," I said stiffly. "And I never said he was a bank robber. He might have been the other one, the one who abandoned his family."

"Whatever," said Kristy, humoring me. "Okay, let's just say this isn't all a product of your imagination. Tell us some more about these criminals. Where are they from? What other names do they go by? Why would they have chosen *Stoneybrook* as a place to hide? Do they have long criminal records, or were these their first crimes?"

"I — I don't remember that much," I confessed, looking down at my hands.

"Maybe the show will be repeated," said Mary Anne helpfully. "Or maybe we could locate a tape."

"Right," said Claudia, unwrapping another Ring-Ding. "And then, if there was more information, maybe we'd have something to go on."

"Does Mr. Finch ever do anything suspicious?" asked Mal. "Like go out at odd hours or wear disguises?"

I shook my head. "Not really," I mumbled. I appreciated how supportive my friends, other than Kristy, were trying to be. But I knew they were just going through the motions. They didn't really believe that Mr. Finch was a criminal.

For that matter, I wasn't sure *I* believed it anymore. My friends weren't convinced by what I'd said, and I couldn't exactly blame them. Maybe I *was* imagining things, because of my fever, or because I was so bored I had to make something exciting happen.

I decided to shut up about it for the time being and investigate some more on my own, without my friends' help. "I guess it was all in my mind," I said sheepishly. "What can you expect from someone who's been burning up with a fever for forty-eight hours?" I gave a little laugh and shrugged my shoulders.

Then the phone rang again, and we moved on to other business. And by the time Kristy declared the meeting adjourned, I was more than ready to go home. I felt tired and a little dizzy, and I was coughing again. I could hardly wait to be back in my own familiar house, the one I'd been so sick of only an hour earlier.

I barely remember the ride back to our neighborhood, or anything Kristy and Charlie

54

talked about. At home, I stumbled out of the car and headed straight inside to the couch.

Mom had come home early — she was making a special effort to be there for dinner each night since I'd been sick — and she and Anna were in the kitchen, talking and laughing while they made dinner. I drifted off for awhile, until Mom shook my shoulder gently and led me to the table.

I didn't eat much of the chicken noodle soup they served me. I was almost too tired to lift the spoon to my mouth. Finally, I gave up. "I'm going to bed," I announced.

My mom was nice enough not to point out that I shouldn't have gone to the meeting. She just kissed my forehead and told me she'd be up later to check on me. Anna gave me a sympathetic look.

I trudged upstairs and down the hall to my room. It was twilight by then, and when I looked out my windows I saw that my neighbors' houses were lit up, including Mr. Finch's.

Immediately, I felt a little surge of energy. I turned off my own light, pulled back the curtains, grabbed the binoculars, and sat near the window to watch. My heart was beating fast.

Soon, though, I was yawning again. Why? Because nothing was happening. Mr. Finch was seated at his kitchen table, eating dinner. A

Healthy Choice microwaved lasagna dinner, to be exact. Hardly the behavior of a hardened criminal.

Maybe I'd been wrong.

Maybe Kristy was right, and I'd seen *Rear Window* too many times.

I started to put down the binoculars, but then something stopped me. Instead, I swept them around to get a good look at the inside of Mr. Finch's kitchen one last time. As I did, I saw something, and I felt a chill run up my spine. (Really! An actual chill!)

Kristy wasn't right after all.

I was.

CHAPTER 7

"Kristy! You won't believe it," I hissed into the phone. (I wasn't exactly eager to have my mom know I'd been spying on the neighbors, so I kept my voice down.)

"What?" Kristy asked. "I thought you told me you were going right to bed."

"I was. Except I had to take one little peek at Mr. Finch's house. And guess what I saw?"

"Mr. Finch holding a machine gun?" Kristy asked.

"*Kristy,*" I said. "Come on, this is serious."

"Okay, what did you see?"

"Well, he was in his kitchen, eating dinner," I began.

"Oh my lord! How suspicious can you get?" interrupted Kristy.

I fell silent. I wasn't even going to give her the satisfaction.

After a couple of seconds, she must have realized how mad I was. "All right, all right, I'm sorry. Go on," Kristy said.

"Well, I looked all around his kitchen, and there on the refrigerator I saw a bunch of drawings. You know, kids' drawings." I paused meaningfully.

"And?" Kristy said. "What does this prove?"

"Don't you see?" I cried, forgetting to keep my voice down. "Here's a guy who supposedly lives all alone, but he has kids' pictures all over his fridge! He must be the guy who abandoned his family!"

"Abby, take it easy. You're jumping to conclusions."

"But —" I began.

"Think about it," she continued. "He could have nieces and nephews or grandchildren. Or maybe he's a schoolteacher. There could be a million reasons why he has those pictures."

"But I've never seen any kids visit him," I said stubbornly.

"Abby," said Kristy. "Listen to me. I think you need some sleep. Go to bed, okay? We'll talk some more in the morning."

I didn't like her tone. She sounded as if she were talking to a two-year-old. But she was right. I *did* need some sleep. Suddenly, I was so exhausted I could hardly hold the phone. "Okay," I agreed. "Good night."

"Good night, Abby," said Kristy. I could picture her shaking her head in amusement. Maybe she was right. Maybe I was just over-tired.

I stumbled into bed without even brushing my teeth or changing into my nightgown. I had a vague memory of my mom coming upstairs later and helping me undress, but it was like a dream. The next thing I knew, it was morning.

And I felt lousy.

Absolutely terrible. I still had bronchitis, plus there must have been some new load of pollen in the air that was making my allergies act up big-time. I couldn't stop sneezing, and sneezing made me cough, and coughing made my throat sore, and — just take my word for it, I was sick as a dog.

The second I opened my eyes, I groaned. Another day home from school, and feeling worse, not better. How could I stand the bore-dom? Then I remembered Mr. Finch.

The minute my mom and Anna left, I slid out of bed and grabbed the binoculars. I aimed them at Mr. Finch's house, but I saw no activity over there at all. Bummer.

I swept the binoculars over the rest of the neighborhood. Then I put them down and yawned. Bo-o-oring. Everybody was off at work or school. Even the birds and squirrels seemed to be settled in for the morning.

Then, out of the corner of my eye, I noticed

movement. I picked up the binoculars again. Yesss! It was him. Mr. Finch. He had come out the back door with a watering can, and he was watering the plants on his patio.

Why wasn't he at work like everybody else?

Did he even have a job?

Maybe he was living off money he'd stolen. . . .

It was time to find out more about Mr. Finch. I put down the binoculars and headed downstairs to find a phone book. Believe it or not, that can be a great place to start when you have a mystery to solve.

Edwards, Falk, Ferber. There it was. Finch. I ran my finger down the listings. Finch, Agnes. Finch, Donna. Finch, Finch, Finch. I never knew there were so many Finches in Stoneybrook. Where was the one I was looking for?

Then I saw it. Finch, O., 2105 Kemp Avenue. That had to be it! Kemp is the next street over. But why didn't the directory show his first name? How annoying. I tried to think of the names "O" could stand for, and could only come up with Oliver and Oscar.

Oliver Finch? Somehow the name didn't fit the man. I went back upstairs and spent some more time monitoring his activities. First he washed some dishes. Then he sat in a recliner near the living room window for awhile, reading the newspaper. After that, he made a phone call, jotting down some notes on a pad that sat on a table near the phone. (I would have loved to be able to read them, but my binoculars weren't quite strong enough.)

Then Mr. Finch disappeared into another part of the house. I watched for awhile longer, but he didn't reappear.

He stayed out of my sight all morning, so I took the opportunity to nap. When I woke up, he still wasn't in view, so I went downstairs and had some chicken noodle soup for lunch. Afterward, I checked on him again, but he was still out of sight. I read for awhile, until I started to feel sleepy again. I didn't really want to nap anymore, since I wouldn't be able to sleep at night if I did. That's when I checked the clock and realized with a little twinge of excitement that it was time for *Mystery Trackers*.

I made a comfy little nest on the couch and settled in to watch. This time, the program had a theme: "Nasty Nannies." It featured three different women who had posed as nannies in order to steal from their employers. I enjoyed the program, even though none of the women reminded me of anyone I knew.

At the end of the show, the 800 number was flashed on the screen again. "Remember," intoned the announcer in that important-sounding voice of his, "you can help. We need your eyes and ears. If there's a criminal in your community, do the right thing — call *Mystery Trackers* today."

Of course! I'd forgotten about their hotline. I threw off my quilt and scrambled for a pen and paper. The credits were rolling, but the number was still displayed on the bottom of the screen. I scribbled it down. Then I grabbed the phone and dialed.

Busy.

Naturally. There were probably three bazillion people out there who thought they'd seen one of the "Nasty Nannies."

I waited a few seconds and punched REDIAL.

Still busy.

I gave up and made myself a cup of tea. After I'd finished it, I tried one more time.

"Hello, *Mystery Trackers*, this is Amy Shapiro speaking. How may I help you?"

"Uh —" Suddenly, I was at a loss for words. Where should I start?

"Have you spotted one of our featured criminals?" prompted the woman on the other end of the line.

"Yes! I mean, I think so," I said. "It was one of the guys on your show earlier this week. He was either the bank robber or the embezzler who abandoned his family."

"Oh, sure," said the woman. "I remember. Did you really spot one of those guys? Cool!" She sounded young — and nearly as excited as I felt.

"Was one of them named Finch?" I asked eagerly.

"Finch? I don't think so," she said. "Let me check the records." She put me on hold, which gave me time to think. That's when I realized I'd made a dumb mistake. I mean, *duh*! Of course the criminal's name wouldn't be Finch. He would have changed his name. That's what criminals do.

"Hi, I'm back." It was Amy Shapiro. "Sorry it took me so long. I'm a summer intern here, and I just started a few days ago. I don't know where everything is yet."

"That's okay," I said. "Did you find the names?"

"Uh-huh," she said. "But neither of them is Finch."

Just what I'd figured.

"The bank robber's name is Harry Bronson, and the other one, the embezzler, is named Arthur Maguire."

I scribbled down the names and thought of another question. "Where were they from?" I asked.

"Let's see," said Amy. "Bronson was from San Francisco. At least, that's where his last robbery was committed. And Maguire, he was from Des Moines, Iowa."

I wrote that down too. "Thanks," I said.

"Anything else I can do?" she asked. "Should

I notify the authorities?" Amy certainly was enthusiastic.

"Oh, no, not yet," I said. "Let's wait until I'm really sure. I mean, I'm pretty sure, but I'm not positive."

"Tell you what," she said. "If you give me your name and address, I'll see if I can round up a copy of that show to send you. That way you can make a positive ID."

A positive ID. The words made me shiver. "Great," I said. This was truly exciting. If I could put a good case together, that would blast my boredom away for good.

Amy and I said good-bye after she'd promised to mail me the tape and I'd promised to call her with any new details about Mr. Finch. Then I headed upstairs for some more Finch-watching.

He was back in the recliner, reading again, or maybe napping, with the newspaper draped over his face. I couldn't tell.

For a second, I had a wild idea. What if I called him up, using the number I'd found in the phone book, and asked for Harry Bronson or Arthur Maguire? I could watch through the binoculars and check the expression on his face when he heard the name. If he looked horrified, I'd know for sure that he was a crook. I reached for the phone.

But he'd also know something. He'd know

that someone was on to him. And then he'd probably move away in the middle of the night and I'd never see him again and my brilliant career as a Mystery Tracker would be over. Hello again, boredom.

I put the phone down.

Then I went back to watching. And waiting.

It was a long, boring afternoon. Mr. Finch didn't do a single interesting thing, unless you count ironing a few shirts.

Eventually, school buses began delivering kids home, and the neighborhood came back to life. When I spotted a certain BSC president hopping off our bus, I waited a few minutes and then dialed Kristy's number. I had a job for her.

CHAPTER 8

Thursday

Okay, Abby, okay. Let's just assume that there is the tiniest possibility that your backyard neighbor is wanted by the authorities. Personally, I still think your fevered brain has gotten the better of you — but since we all love a mystery, I hereby declare this an official BSC investigation.

Kristy's entry in the mystery notebook wasn't exactly supportive, but seeing it made me happy anyway. She'd brought the notebook to my house to prove that she was ready to play along with my "fantasies" about Mr. Finch.

What's the mystery notebook? Well, it's another of Kristy's great ideas. See, the BSC members have been involved in solving quite a few mysteries. And when you're collecting clues and speculating about suspects, you need a place in which to keep notes. I guess the club members used to write stuff down just about anywhere — on the backs of their hands or on napkins from a pizza place — but sometime before I joined the club Kristy came up with the idea for the mystery notebook. Ever since then our investigations have been a lot more organized.

Kristy's entry went on to tell about some sleuthing she did that same day, under pressure from me.

"Come on, Kristy, *please*?" I begged. We were sitting in my room, on the window seat.

"Don't you know it's a federal crime to tamper with somebody's mail?" she asked, folding her arms across her chest. "I could end up in prison. Is that what you want?"

I shook my head. "Of course not," I said.

"But you wouldn't be tampering. You'd just be peeking. For one second. What's the harm?"

Kristy frowned. "He might come home," she said.

"I really don't think he will. I'm starting to know his schedule. He hardly ever goes out, but when he does, he always stays away for a couple of hours."

I picked up the binoculars and went to the other window. "And I can tell that the mail is there," I said. "Kristy, *please*? This is our big chance."

"Our big chance to find ourselves in big trouble. And all for what? To find out your neighbor's name? There must be an easier way."

There wasn't. Not that I could think of. I'd tried the phone book, but that hadn't worked. All I was asking Kristy to do was to ride her bike around to the front of Mr. Finch's house and crack open his mailbox, which stood at the end of his driveway. I could see it from my window. Earlier, the little red flag on it had been up, which was a signal to the letter carrier that there was mail inside waiting to be picked up. Now the flag was down, which meant that the letter carrier had stopped by. Mr. Finch had gone out about fifteen minutes earlier, and I hadn't seen him check the mail as he drove away. That meant that this was our golden opportunity. If we ("we" meaning Kristy, since going outside would be sure to activate my allergies and keep me sneezing for hours) could just take one quick look at Mr. Finch's mail, we could find out what that "O" stood for. And knowing the alias he was using would be an excellent next step. I had already told Kristy about my phone call with Amy Shapiro.

"Okay, if you don't want to do it, I can't make you," I said in a depressed tone. "If only I wasn't too sick to go out. Maybe I should just risk it. . . ."

Kristy threw up her hands. "I'll do it, I'll do it," she said. "But keep an eye on me with the binoculars, okay? And if you see his car coming, you'd better give me some kind of signal so I can make a clean getaway."

I nodded. This was more like it. "I'll wave to you," I said. "Will that work?"

She shook her head. "I can't watch you all the time."

I thought for a second, then remembered something. "Hold on," I said. I went to Anna's room and rummaged around in her desk. When I came back I was holding my dad's harmonica. I stood near Kristy and blew through the instrument, hard. The sound that came out was not exactly "She'll Be Comin' Round the Mountain."

Kristy covered her ears and grimaced. "That ought to do it."

Five minutes later, I was watching through the binoculars as Kristy pulled her bike up to Mr. Finch's mailbox. She looked each way to be sure nobody was coming, then glanced up at me and gave a tiny wave. I waved back.

Then she reached forward and opened the mailbox. I could see through the binoculars that a piece of mail was sticking out. Kristy checked it, then looked toward my window and gave me the thumbs-up sign. She must have seen Mr. Finch's first name. Yesss!

I put down the binoculars, assuming Kristy was going to close the mailbox and pedal away. Instead, she reached a hand deeper into the box. I put the binoculars up to my eyes again. "Kristy," I murmured, "what are you doing?"

Kristy seemed to be tugging at something. Was she nuts? Now she *was* tampering.

Suddenly, she stepped backward — and a whole pile of mail shot out of the box and landed on the ground. "Oh, no." I groaned. I swept the binoculars each way, looking for an approaching car. My free hand tightened around the harmonica.

But the street was empty, and Kristy acted fast, scooping up the letters and stuffing them quickly but carefully back into the box. Closing it, she looked up at me and grinned, swiping a hand across her forehead. I could almost hear her sigh with relief. Then she rode off.

Moments later, I heard her thumping up the stairs. "Otto!" she was crying. "His name is Otto!"

Otto Finch. Interesting.

Kristy burst into my room and collapsed on my bed. "Whew!" she said. "Don't ever make me do that again."

"Why did you pull everything out?" I asked.

"I didn't mean to," she explained. "It just happened. I was trying to wedge out this one letter, to see the return address. But the whole pile flew out at me!"

"So, did you see where the letter came from?" I asked, curious.

She nodded. And suddenly she looked very serious. "Iowa," she said. "It came from Des Moines, Iowa."

I looked at Kristy. "I'm going to call Amy Shapiro again." I reached for the phone.

Amy was very interested to hear that my neighbor was from Iowa. Then I asked her if Otto Finch was one of Maguire's known aliases. She put me on hold while she checked. When she came back she told me that the name didn't show up on his records. She sounded a little less excited.

My excitement died down too. I'd thought we were on the brink of catching a criminal, but maybe not. Maybe the whole thing was in my head. At least it was in Kristy's head now too. I had company.

Friday

Well, nobody can say I didn't try. I guess I can't blame Sergeant Johnson for being a little tired of mystery Trackers.

Mary Anne had stopped in at the police station downtown for an informal chat with a friend of the BSC, Sergeant Johnson. We've worked on more than one mystery with him, and he knows we're good detectives. Mary Anne thought she'd mention my suspicions about Mr. Finch to him and see what he said.

He didn't seem too excited to hear about the criminal in our midst. "Mary Anne," he said gently, shaking his head. "I have to tell you that shows like that one sometimes do more harm than good. I'll be glad to run a check on your Mr. Finch, but I can almost guarantee you that he'll come up clean."

Mary Anne nodded. "That's what I think too," she told him. "But it doesn't hurt to check, does it?"

He shook his head. "Not as long as the person doesn't know you're checking. Some people might not be too happy about being spied on, you know," he said, giving her a Look.

Mary Anne thanked him and told him she understood.

Friday

Hey, dudes! Serfing the net is awesome! Too true. It took us awhile, but we found some interesting stuff. I wonder what Abby will think of the pictures.

Claudia and Stacey were pretty excited about their first experience with cyber-sleuthing. (Translation: playing detective with a computer.) After hearing Kristy's update of the case at Friday's BSC meeting (which I skipped because I was feeling too rotten), they cornered Janine and talked her into letting them use her computer — and her computer skills.

Stacey had heard that you could look up anybody's name on the Internet and find out where that person lives. Most people do it to find old college roommates or trace long-lost relatives, but Stacey figured you could catch a thief that way too. Why not look up Otto Finch and see what information was available on him?

"That may be possible," Janine said when they'd explained what they wanted to do. "I'm intrigued enough to help you try." With a few taps on the keyboard, a squeal from the modem, and a few more taps, she'd entered the Internet. After searching around for awhile, she found the correct site. She stood up to let Stacey and Claudia do the rest.

"Just type in his name," she told them, "and see what comes up."

Claudia started toward the keyboard, then stopped. "You'd better do it, Stace," she said. "I'll probably spell it wrong."

Stacey tapped in the letters: Otto Finch. The computer made some "thinking" noises while the girls waited eagerly. Finally, an answer came up. It showed an Otto Finch living at 2015 Kemp Ave. in Stoneybrook, Connecticut.

Stacey and Claudia looked at each other. "Bummer," said Claudia. "Looks like everything checks out."

"Wait, though," Stacey said slowly, thinking. "What if that's not really his name?"

"You mean —" Claudia began.

"Let's try something just for kicks," said Stacey. "Is the mystery notebook in your room?"

Claudia ran to find it.

"What were those names?" asked Stacey.

"The ones the *Mystery Tracker* intern gave Abby?"

Claudia flipped the pages. "Let's see," she said. "Oh, here they are. Harry Bronson and Arthur Maguire."

Stacey entered one name and then the other. "Pay dirt!" she cried as the computer screen filled, first with information about Maguire and then with a page on Bronson.

Janine leaned over her shoulder. "There's even a Web site where you can download pictures," she pointed out. She showed Stacey how to find it, and within ten minutes she and Claudia were holding two blurry pictures that Janine had helped them print out.

"Hmm," said Claudia.

"Hmm," said Stacey.

Both of them were staring at the second picture that had popped out of the printer. The first one, which they'd glanced at and dismissed, was of Harry Bronson. He was a big, muscle-bound guy with a shaved head — hardly a match for Mr. Finch. But Arthur Maguire was a different story.

"He's definitely not *identical*," said Stacey carefully. She and Claudia had seen Mr. Finch once or twice when they were visiting me.

"No," said Claudia. "But I think I can see what Abby's talking about." She squinted at the picture. "Maybe."

CHAPTER 9

Saturday

Well, we almost had a record on our hands — the record for the most hours passed without incident or accident of any type while in the company of Jackie Kodowsky. It was a pretty awesome day, even if Jackie won't make it into the Guinness Book of Records. He certainly deserves an E for Effort!

The day after she saw Sergeant Johnson, Mary Anne had a sitting job with the Rodowsky brothers: Shea, who's nine; Jackie (the Walking Disaster, remember?), who's seven; and Archie, who's only four. All three boys are freckle-faced redheads.

The Wednesday before, Kristy had been sitting for the boys when they first decided to form a team for the go-cart races. That day, they hadn't had time to begin construction of their vehicle, but by the time Mary Anne arrived on Saturday, they were ready to start building.

There was only one problem.

None of them had a clue about what their go-cart should look like.

When Mrs. Rodowsky showed her into the garage, Mary Anne found three downcast boys sitting in the middle of a carefully arranged pile of parts: wheels, axles, plywood, two-by-fours, nuts and bolts. Shea was hunched over a magazine, looking puzzled.

"You guys seem to be all set," said Mary Anne. "Why haven't you started building?"

Shea shrugged. "We don't know where to begin," he said. He looked a little upset. "We have this article Mom found, but I can't figure out what it's talking about."

Suddenly, Mary Anne understood. Shea is

dyslexic, and while he's great at some things, like figures and measurements, he has a hard time reading and following directions. And Jackie and Archie, both younger, were probably looking to Shea for guidance.

"Maybe you need to see a real go-cart," Mary Anne said. "One that's being built right now. Would that help?"

"Definitely!" said Shea eagerly. "Can we go over to the Pikes'? I know the triplets are building one."

"We don't have to go that far," Mary Anne said. "There's a team working right here in this neighborhood."

"There is?" asked Jackie. "Who?"

"The Glory Girls," said Mary Anne, remembering Stacey's and Mal's notes. "Charlotte, Vanessa, and Becca. They were working over at the Pikes', but I think the garage there became a little too crowded for two teams. Anyway, I hear they've moved their operation to Charlotte's house. Should I give them a call and see if we can go over?" Mary Anne knew that Jessi was sitting for Charlotte that afternoon, and that she'd probably brought Becca with her. "Or do you want to have lunch first?"

Shea and Jackie glanced at each other. "Um, how about if we go after lunch?" Shea asked. "Are you going to make us some sandwiches?"

"I was planning to," said Mary Anne.

"Good," said Shea. "Let's eat first, then."

Mary Anne shrugged and agreed. She headed for the kitchen to put lunch together, noticing that Shea started whispering to Jackie even before she'd left the garage. The Rodowsky boys were up to something, but Mary Anne couldn't guess what it was. She didn't even try. Instead, she just crossed her fingers and hoped that, whatever it was, Jackie wouldn't break anything.

Ten minutes later, as she was stacking sandwiches on a plate, the phone rang. It was Jessi. "What are those boys up to?" she demanded.

"Shea and Jackie?" asked Mary Anne, realizing she hadn't heard their voices in awhile.

"And Archie," answered Jessi. "They're sneaking around, thinking we don't see them. But we do! They think they're being subtle, but it's obvious what they're up to."

Mary Anne laughed. "I bet they're spying," she said. "They want to know how to build a go-cart, but they're too embarrassed to ask a bunch of girls."

Jessi giggled. "That's silly," she said. "Charlotte and Vanessa and Becca would be glad to help them."

"They're already helping them," said Mary Anne. "If the boys have had even a glimpse of their go-cart, they'll probably be full of ideas."

Mary Anne hung up and finished making lunch. Then she put everything on a tray and brought it out to the garage. "Jac-kie, Ar-chie, Shea!" she called out the open door. "Lunch is ready."

The boys came running. Their faces were flushed and their eyes were bright with excitement.

"So, have you come up with any ideas?" Mary Anne asked innocently.

"Lots!" said Jackie. "Now we know how you put the frame together and attach it to the wheels." He grabbed a sandwich and started eating.

"So you figured out what the magazine was saying?" asked Mary Anne, hiding a smile.

"Um — right!" said Shea. "Right, the magazine." He picked it up and leafed through it.

"And we saw Char —" Archie began, but his brothers shushed him.

"Have a sandwich, Archie," said Shea.

"And Vaness —" Archie began.

Jackie shoved a glass of milk into his brother's hand. "And some milk," he said. "Drink up!"

"So," said Mary Anne, deciding to let the boys have their secret, "who's going to be the driver of this awesome go-cart?"

"Me! Me!" cried Jackie. "I want to."

"Are you out of your mind?" asked Shea.

80

"You'd crash the thing in a minute. You've already totaled two bikes."

"Totaled?" asked Mary Anne.

"You know, like a car crash. When the car is completely wrecked, they say it's totaled," Shea explained.

"I could drive," Archie suggested happily.

"I don't think so," Shea said gently. "But you can be in the pit crew. You know, the guys who have all the tools and fix the race cars when they break. No, I'll probably drive."

Jackie looked deflated. "I know I could do it without crashing," he murmured. "If I really try, I can be careful."

And for the rest of the day, Jackie set out to prove himself to Shea. Mary Anne had never seen Jackie move so slowly or carefully. "It was as if he had become his own opposite," she told us later. "Like the Walking Disaster side of him is really his evil twin or something."

Jackie did everything right. He followed Shea's directions to the letter as they began putting their go-cart together. He sawed through boards without sawing through his own clothes or the old kitchen table he was leaning on. He hammered nails without banging his thumb. And when he almost — *almost* — knocked over a jar filled with screws, he caught it just in time, before Archie was covered in a shower of hardware.

Mary Anne watched with growing admiration. Maybe Jackie was maturing. Maybe he'd finally learned how to tame his Walking Disaster side. Maybe sitting for the Rodowskys wouldn't be so dangerous anymore.

Then, toward the end of the afternoon, Shea made an announcement.

"We still have to attach the steering mechanism and the brake," he told his brothers. "But so far, I think we've done a terrific job. Jackie, I take it back. I think you might just be the perfect driver for this go-cart."

Jackie beamed. "Wow! Really? Cool." He and Shea gave each other a high five. Then Archie wanted to give him one too, so all three brothers spent a few minutes congratulating each other.

Then Shea made a big mistake.

He opened a can of paint.

"We might as well put a first coat onto the main part of the go-cart," he said. "That way, once we attach the last parts and put on another coat, she'll be ready to roll. We'll have time for some practice runs."

Eagerly, the three boys began to paint. Shea had found an old can of orange paint that his dad had used to touch up their driveway basketball hoop, and the color looked great.

They'd opened the door of the garage for ventilation, and a cool breeze blew around, keeping the smell of paint to a minimum. All was quiet and peaceful as the boys worked.

Then, suddenly, Jackie let out a whoop. "Hey!" he yelled. "What do you think you're doing?" He stood up quickly and pointed, kicking the can of paint as he moved. Over it went, flowing onto Archie's sneakers. Archie looked up, surprised, as orange paint puddled around his feet.

"Aww, Jackie, why did you have to do that?" asked Shea. "You were doing so well."

"Do you expect me to stand for it when those girls spy on us?" asked Jackie, waving his arms. "I just saw all three of them peeking around the corner of the garage. They're trying to steal our secrets so they can win the race!"

Mary Anne looked from an outraged Jackie to a head-shaking Shea to an orange-paint-drenched Archie — and all she could do was try her best not to laugh.

CHAPTER 10

"I don't believe you!" Kristy said. "Aren't you tired of spying yet?"

It was Sunday afternoon, and Kristy had come by to visit. She'd caught me sitting at the window, binoculars glued to my eyes, staring out at Mrs. Porter's house. (Mr. Finch was out, or else I'd have been staring at him.) It was a drizzly, gray day, and I was still feeling pretty lousy. "What else is there to do?" I asked. "Anyway, it's fun. Want to look?" I offered her the binoculars. "Mrs. Porter is cooking up some kind of stew. Probably eye of newt, or at least that's what Karen would think."

"I'm not interested," said Kristy. "It's rude to spy on people." Then I saw her glance at Mrs. Porter's house and knew that, despite her words, she was tempted.

"But you learn so much," I said. "I mean, I can tell you all kinds of secrets about people in this neighborhood."

"Abby!" said Kristy, looking shocked. She paused for a second. "Like — like what, for example?" Her curiosity was getting the better of her.

"Like, the Korman kids are building a go-cart, and I have a feeling it's going to be very fast. I'd bet on them to win the race, and none of the other teams even knows that Melody and Bill are entering!"

"Interesting," Kristy said. "What else?"

"I think Shannon has a secret admirer," I said. "There's this boy who rides his bike past her house at least twice a day. He always tries to look cool, as if he's just in the neighborhood by chance, but I can tell by the way he slows down as he passes her yard that he's looking for her."

Kristy smiled. "I wonder if she knows," she said.

"And Mr. Papadakis is building a shed in their side yard, and based on what she's been putting out for the garbage collectors, Mrs. Papadakis must be cleaning out all the closets in the house," I continued. "And Ms. Fielding just bought five new rosebushes, and —"

Kristy was looking perturbed. "Wait a minute," she said. "If you know all this stuff about everyone else in the neighborhood, you must know stuff about my family too."

"Um," I said, stalling.

"Go on." Kristy put her hands on her hips. "Tell me. What's going on at *my* house?" She still sounded curious, but I heard something else in her voice too.

I decided to tread carefully. "We-ell," I began slowly, "I know that Watson's been thinking about planting some new trees, because I've seen him pacing around in the yard with the man from the nursery."

"Uh-huh," said Kristy. "And?"

"And Karen seems pretty bummed — probably about Andrew being gone?" I added, knowing that this wouldn't be news to Kristy.

Kristy frowned. "I know," she said. "What else?"

"That new girlfriend of Charlie's? I'm not sure she's as crazy about him as he is about her."

Kristy's eyes narrowed. "How can you possibly know that?"

I shrugged. "It's just that she, um, makes faces when his back is turned sometimes. You know, rolling her eyes and stuff."

"Abby!" Kristy said. "How much time have you spent spying on my family?" She shook her head. "I think you've gone a little too far with this. I mean, to know all these details —" She broke off. "Wait a minute," she said, staring out the window. "Is that the guy you've seen riding by Shannon's house? I think I know who he is. Pass me the binoculars."

I grinned and handed them over. Kristy had caught the bug.

She watched the boy until she realized that she didn't know him after all, then swept the binoculars around to check out the other neighborhood action. "What about our so-called criminal, Mr. Finch?" she asked, directing her gaze toward his house.

"Oh my lord!" I said, smacking my head. "I can't believe I forgot to tell you. The tape came in the mail yesterday!"

"The tape?"

"You know, of the show. Of the first *Mystery Trackers* show I saw. Remember the intern, Amy, who was going to send me a tape? Well, she did."

Kristy looked impressed. "Cool," she said. "Have you watched it yet?"

"Are you kidding? I've seen it twice. No — three times. I would have watched it again, but I don't want Mom and Anna to start asking questions."

"And?" asked Kristy.

"And I really think he could be him," I said excitedly. "I mean I think Mr. Finch might really be Arthur Maguire."

"Which one was Maguire?" Kristy asked. "The bank robber or the embezzler?"

"The embezzler."

"Oh, right. The one from Iowa."

"The one who abandoned his family," I said, nodding. "I'm telling you, this guy is a dead ringer for Mr. Finch. And there are other clues too, like the furniture —"

"Furniture?" she interrupted, holding up a hand. "Hold on there. Maybe I should take a look at this show." She held up the binoculars again and checked Mr. Finch's house. "Still not home," she murmured. "Let's go to the videotape!"

We hurried downstairs. Fortunately, my mom and Anna were out. I didn't want to have to explain anything to them. I pulled the tape out from its hiding place behind the others we own and stuck it into the VCR. Kristy and I settled in on the couch to watch.

The tape was so familiar to me by then that I could practically recite along with the narration. But it was Kristy's first time, so I tried to keep quiet and let her watch.

The segment on Arthur Maguire opened with a picture of his employee card from the last place he'd worked. "See?" I asked. "See what I mean?"

"Shh," said Kristy, concentrating. The announcer was talking about Arthur Maguire, and how he'd always seemed like an upstanding citizen. There were a couple of interviews with coworkers and neighbors who said that he was polite enough, even though he "kept to himself." Then there was some footage of his tearful wife, who talked about how shocked she'd been when he disappeared. In the background, two young kids — a girl and a boy, maybe six and eight — squabbled over a box of cereal.

Then there was a series of pictures of Maguire: In some he looked younger, in some, older; in some he had a mustache and in others he didn't; in some he looked serious and in some he was laughing. As the pictures flashed by, the announcer talked about what Maguire had done. He'd disappeared with over twenty thousand dollars of other people's money!

Kristy whistled. "How could he have thought he would get away with that?" she asked.

"Wait, there's more," I said. The last part of the segment was coming up, the part I'd paid the most attention to. It was a family video, made on Arthur Maguire's birthday. There were shots of him blowing out candles, opening presents, and listening to his family sing "Happy Birthday." Through it all he looked content, and totally normal. As if he were any regular American dad.

"What a creep," Kristy muttered as the last images faded. "How could he cut out on his family that way?"

Her voice sounded a little thick. I looked over and saw that her face was tight. Suddenly, I realized she must be thinking of her own dad, who had abandoned her and her mom and her brothers so many years before. Of course, he hadn't stolen money from them, but I could see why she'd have especially hard feelings toward Arthur Maguire.

"So, what do you think?" I asked gently, trying to change the subject a little. "Doesn't he look like Mr. Finch?"

"Absolutely," said Kristy. "I have to apologize for doubting you. The two of them could be twin brothers."

Yesss! Finally, I'd convinced someone. "And you know what?" I asked. "The furniture he has in his house now is just like the furniture in the home movie. So Finch also has the same taste as Maguire. There's even a vase on the hall table that looks like he might have taken it with him when he left."

"Whoa!" said Kristy. "Let's go check that out." I could tell she was dying to grab those binoculars again. She'd forgotten any objection she'd once had to spying.

We headed back upstairs. "And the kids," I said. "Those two kids would be just the right ages to produce that refrigerator art. I've seen a lot of pictures on a lot of fridges, and I know what kids draw."

"Right," said Kristy. "Like, at six they all draw houses with smoke coming out of the chimney. And at eight they're drawing horses, if they're girls —"

"And rocket ships, if they're boys," I chimed in. "That's exactly what's on his fridge. A drawing of a house and a picture of a rocket ship. I figure Patty drew the house and Joseph drew the rocket." (Patty and Joseph were the names of Arthur Maguire's kids. We'd learned that from the video.)

"I have a great idea," said Kristy, picking up the binoculars and focusing on Mr. Finch's house.

"I bet I know what it is, and the answer is no," I said. "The binoculars aren't quite good enough to let us read the signatures on those pictures."

"Bummer," mumbled Kristy, who was sweeping the binoculars from room to room in Mr. Finch's house. "Well, then, we'll have to figure out some other way to catch him."

Behind her, I raised a victorious fist in the air. I'd convinced Kristy. Now maybe it was time to convince the authorities.

CHAPTER 11

"Take my advice, Abby. Forget about this and go back to bed. You sound like you need some rest!"

"But Sergeant Johnson," I pleaded. "I'm telling you, it's not just my imagination."

It was Monday morning. I was home from school again — my cough had worsened in the night, and I'd hardly slept — and I was on the phone with my favorite "authority," Sergeant Johnson. I'd called him first thing, as soon as my mom and Anna had left for the day. Fortunately, he wasn't currently working the night shift, which meant he was in his office.

Sergeant Johnson is a really good guy. He's not the kind of adult who belittles kids or doesn't take them seriously. And he knows that the BSC members are good detectives. (He's handsome too, by the way — for a grown-up. He's tall, with black hair and swimming-pool-blue eyes.) But this was one case he thought we should forget about.

I'd called to tell him about receiving the tape from *Mystery Trackers* and how watching it had confirmed my suspicion that Mr. Finch and Arthur Maguire were one and the same. "He even has the same taste in furniture," I blurted out, feeling silly as soon as I'd said it. Sergeant Johnson would think I was working too hard to make a point.

"Furniture?" he asked, clearly puzzled. Then he realized what I was saying. "Abby, I warned Mary Anne about spying on your neighbors. You'd better watch your step."

"Never mind about the furniture," I said quickly. "But the two of them really do look alike. And I'm not the only one who thinks so. Kristy agrees one hundred percent."

"Does she, now," Sergeant Johnson said.

I was beginning to feel he was humoring me. "Really!" I said. Then I broke out into a fit of coughing.

That's when he told me to go back to bed.

"But didn't you tell Mary Anne you would run a check on Mr. Finch?" I asked. "When are you going to do that?" I knew I was pushing my luck. I hoped Sergeant Johnson would chalk up my behavior to the fact that I was sick.

"I've already done it," he said gently.

"You have?" I asked, nearly shrieking. "Why didn't you tell me?"

"You didn't give me a chance. Anyway, there's nothing to tell. The check came up clear."

For a second I was speechless. I couldn't believe what I was hearing. "Clear?" I asked finally.

"Clear," Sergeant Johnson repeated firmly. "He has a legitimate driver's license with no criminal record on the holder. And the state of Iowa is very good about keeping up their records."

"Iowa?" I repeated. "Wait a second. Are you saying that Otto Finch is from Iowa?"

Sergeant Johnson raised an eyebrow. Don't ask me how I could tell over the phone. I just could. "That's correct, Abby. And as far as I can remember from my police training, there's no law against being from Iowa." Now he was smiling too. That came through the phone lines crystal clear.

"But don't you see?" I asked impatiently. "Arthur Maguire is from Iowa too. Des Moines, Iowa."

"Uh-huh," said Sergeant Johnson. "And so are thousands of other people." I heard the sound of shuffling papers and knew he had started to tune me out. He was cleaning his desk as we talked.

"Sergeant Johnson —" I began.

"Listen to me, Abby. I promise to keep an eye on this Mr. Finch of yours. But so far he has not done a single illegal thing. And in this country, people are considered innocent until proven guilty. Now, I would really rather not field any complaints from him about neighborhood teenagers spying on his comings and goings. So I think you'd better lay off for awhile. Understand?"

I was silent.

"Abby? Come on, now. You know it's not that I don't value your detective work. It's just that this time . . . this time —"

"You think I'm off my rocker," I said.

"I wasn't going to put it that way. The fact is, I'm really just too busy to spend any more time on this today." I heard papers shuffling in the background again.

"I understand," I said. "Thanks for running that check. Good-bye, Sergeant Johnson."

"Good-bye, Abby. Hope you feel better soon."

I hung up, feeling rotten. Why was it that nobody believed me? Well, Kristy did. But only because she'd seen things with her own eyes. Maybe that's what it would take. Maybe I'd have to convince Sergeant Johnson to come over and view the tape, then take another look at Mr. Finch. I reached for the phone, then pulled my hand back. Sergeant Johnson had made it perfectly clear that he'd rather not hear from me again anytime in the near future.

I couldn't believe Sergeant Johnson didn't make anything of the fact that Otto Finch was from Iowa. It seemed like more than just a major coincidence to me. I groaned, frustrated. Suddenly, I felt too tired to stand up for another second. (I'd been talking on the kitchen phone.) I sat down at the table with my head in my hands. Detective work was supposed to be fun, wasn't it? But this case was stalled, and there was nothing I could do about it.

I glanced at the clock. Ten minutes after nine. I wasn't hungry, but I knew I should eat something. I spent a few minutes rummaging around in the fridge, then sat down again and spooned some black cherry yogurt into my mouth. After I'd eaten half the container, I gave up. I was too sleepy even to hold the spoon.

I tidied up by putting away the yogurt and rinsing off the spoon in the sink. Then I stumbled upstairs to my room. Out of habit, I glanced out the window to see what the neighbors were doing. A movement at Mr. Finch's house caught my eye, and I picked up the binoculars to take a better look.

He was in his backyard, hanging out laundry. Two plain white T-shirts, a pair of tan slacks, several pairs of black socks, and a blue button-down shirt, to be exact. Mr. Finch was not the most exciting dresser in the world.

I pulled a chair to a spot near the window and settled in with the binoculars. Mr. Finch wasn't doing anything suspicious, but what would it hurt to keep tabs on him? I thought of Sergeant Johnson's warning against spying and felt uncomfortable for a moment. But the moment passed, and soon I was watching every move my neighbor made.

Until I fell asleep, that is.

Oh, yes, even spymasters need to snooze. The binoculars fell into my lap, my chin dropped to my chest, and I was dozing, big-time.

I think I slept for almost two hours, right there in that chair. It's a rocking chair, the one my mom used when she was nursing Anna and me, so it's pretty comfortable. But still, I was more than a little stiff when I woke up.

I don't know what woke me. Maybe it was a bird or an airplane passing overhead. All I know is that it took me quite a while to wipe the fog from my brain. I stretched and yawned and coughed until I began to feel a little less muddled.

Then I lifted the binoculars to my eyes. After all, I was still seated by the window. Why not check on Mr. Finch? (Okay, I admit it. I was a tiny bit addicted to spying.)

He wasn't in the backyard anymore or in the living room. But — "Hey," I said in a low voice. Mr. Finch was in his kitchen. And he wasn't doing dishes.

What was he doing, you ask? Good question. But you probably won't believe the answer.

He was burning things. In the sink.

First he burned what looked like a passport-sized book. A bankbook? Then he burned some photographs. I could see the colors melting as the fire consumed them, but I couldn't see what — or who — the subjects were.

Now, if this wasn't suspicious behavior, what was?

I almost ran for the phone. Sergeant Johnson would have to listen to me this time. But then I imagined the conversation. "Abby," he'd say. "It's true that burning things in the sink is odd behavior. But it's certainly not illegal. Would you have me burst into Mr. Finch's house and arrest him for it?"

I couldn't call Sergeant Johnson, that was clear. But I had to talk to someone. So I called Amy Shapiro at *Mystery Trackers*. She was properly impressed. In fact, she was pretty excited. "I just know we're going to break this case!" she said. "Listen, Abby, you sit tight and keep watching him. I'm going to alert the authorities who are working on the Maguire case. I think it's time."

Yes. It *was* time.

When I hung up, I felt another wave of exhaustion hit me. This time, I lay down on my bed and stretched out. And this time, I slept for more than a couple of hours. In fact, I slept straight through until later that afternoon, when Kristy showed up after school.

CHAPTER 12

Okay, here's the part where I give a confession and a warning.

The confession? What Kristy and I did next was not entirely brilliant.

The warning? Don't try this at home. You'll see why.

When Kristy woke me up that afternoon (she'd let herself in, since Mom was still at work and Anna was at a rehearsal), I was still pretty groggy, but it didn't take me long to snap out of it and fill her in on what was happening with Mr. Finch.

Kristy listened carefully, interrupting with a few questions, as I told her about my phone call to Sergeant Johnson. She seemed as frustrated as I was about the fact that Mr. Finch's license had come up clear, and that Sergeant Johnson refused to see how serious we were.

Then I told her what I'd seen just before I fell asleep. Her eyes widened. "You're kidding," she said when I described Mr. Finch's behavior. She smacked a fist into her open hand. "He must be burning evidence. Maybe he knows someone's on to him!"

"How could he know?" I asked. I'd been very careful when I was spying, and I knew Mr. Finch had never seen me or my binoculars.

"I don't know," said Kristy. "Maybe he's just nervous. Maybe his guilty conscience won't leave him alone." She was pacing. "So, go on. What happened next?"

I told her about calling Amy Shapiro.

"Excellent," said Kristy. "Great. How long did she say it would take them to respond?"

"Um," I said, trying to remember. The call was a little hazy. My mind was still very foggy. "I don't think she said."

"So it may be awhile," Kristy muttered, almost to herself. "That means we're the only ones on the case for now." She was still pacing. I lay on my bed, too exhausted to move my head back and forth to follow her.

"What if he's preparing to skip town?" Kristy wondered aloud. "What if he disappears before they can catch him?" She smacked her fist into her hand again. "We have to do something."

"Like what?" I asked. I was way too tired to come up with any fancy plans.

"Like . . ." Kristy paced a little faster. "Like,

okay, first, we make sure he's not at home." She began to talk faster and faster, as if her mouth could hardly keep up with her brain. "Then, I run over to his house and do some snooping. I won't go in or anything. That would be illegal and could be dangerous. I'll just look into the kitchen windows and check the names on those drawings. If they're signed Patty and Joseph, we'll *know* we're right. And Sergeant Johnson will have to believe us."

"Kristy!" I gasped. "Are you sure this is a good idea?"

She shrugged. "Do you have a better one?"

I shook my head. "I guess not." My foggy brain was trying to tell me something, and finally it came through. "But — but how are we going to make sure he's not at home?"

"Piece of cake," said Kristy. "I rented *Rear Window* last night. In the movie they want to check out the guy's apartment. So what do they do?"

I thought for a second, foggily. Then a little light went on. "They call him!" I said. "They don't say who they are, but they tell him to meet them at some bar or something."

"Right," said Kristy. "And their mistake was that they let him know they were on to him. We won't do that. We'll just pretend we're calling from the library or something."

"You mean you're going to —" I was having

a hard time keeping up with Kristy's thought process.

By the time I'd finished my sentence, Kristy had ducked out into the hall and returned to my room, carrying the cordless phone and a phone book. She looked up Otto Finch's number in the book and punched it in, reciting the numbers out loud as she did.

I watched, paralyzed, as she calmly waited for him to pick up. When he did, she put on a very adult-sounding, nasal voice. "Mr. Finch?" she asked. "I'm calling from the phone company. We're having some trouble with your bill — a matter of some calls to Iowa?"

I drew in a breath. Kristy just grinned at me. She was on a roll. "Perhaps we could work it out most easily if you were to come down to the office," she suggested smoothly. "I'm available right now. Just ask for Ms. Purdy." She gave directions to the phone company building, which is in downtown Stoneybrook. "Wonderful," she said, maintaining that voice perfectly. "I'll see you in about fifteen minutes, then." She hung up and thrust a fist into the air. "Yesss!" she cried. "He bought it — totally."

I was speechless. I couldn't believe Kristy was doing this. "I thought you hated prank phone calls," I said.

"Sure, when somebody's ordering pizzas to be delivered to unsuspecting people," she agreed. "But this is different. This is all in the name of justice." She grabbed the binoculars and trained them on Mr. Finch's house. "He's looking for his car keys!" she crowed.

Then she turned to me. "Okay, we don't have long. It will only take him about fifteen minutes or so to drive down there and find out there's no such person as Ms. Purdy." She checked her watch. "So, what we need to do is figure out a secret signal. Something you can do to let me know he's on his way back, if you see his car coming down the street."

"Should we stick with the harmonica idea we used last time?" I asked.

Kristy nodded. "That'll work," she said. "Just be loud."

"Like this?" I asked, before blowing with all my might.

It was *really* loud. Kristy covered her ears. "That should be fine," she mumbled. Then she glanced out the window. "He's leaving!"

I heard the slam of a car door and a motor starting.

"That's it," said Kristy. "I'm out of here." She grinned and gave me the thumbs-up. "Wish me luck," she said.

I tried to grin back. "Good luck," I replied.

She was out the door before I could say another word. For a moment, I wondered if I should follow her. I wasn't at all convinced that she was doing the right thing, but still, should she be doing it on her own? I stood up — and started wheezing a little. "Oh, great," I said between breaths. "An asthma attack. That's all I need." It wasn't a bad one, but I needed my inhaler. I headed to the bathroom to find it, but when I got there, I felt better — no inhaler needed. By the time I returned to the window, Kristy was already in Mr. Finch's yard.

She was creeping carefully across that perfectly trimmed lawn, looking to the right and left and checking behind her every few steps. From where I stood, even without the binoculars, I could tell she was nervous. And excited. Kristy was on a mission.

I just hoped it wasn't Mission Impossible.

I picked up the binoculars for a better look and tracked Kristy's progress across the lawn. Within seconds, she'd reached the patio. I saw her lean down to check on the book Mr. Finch had left near his lounge chair — nosy thing! — then continue past the sliding glass doors that led to the living room.

Finally, she reached the kitchen window. She turned and waved at me, and I waved back, even though I was unsure if she could see me. Then she stood on her tiptoes and, making a tunnel with both hands around her face, peeked inside.

Just then, I heard a car. My heart began to

thud, and I swung the binoculars around to see who was coming. Was Mr. Finch a faster driver than we'd thought? Was he coming home already?

No. I caught sight of the car and saw that it was a blue minivan, not a white sedan like Mr. Finch's. My heart began to slow a little.

Then I swept the binoculars back to check on Kristy. She was standing in front of the window, her back to it so she was facing me. And she was beaming. She nodded and grinned.

I knew what that meant. Those pictures had the signatures we were looking for.

I grinned back, and then motioned to her to keep moving. Now that we knew for sure that Mr. Finch was Mr. Maguire, it was time for Kristy to head back to my house. The sooner she was out of that yard, the better. As she started to walk, I felt a wave of relief roll over me. Then I started wheezing again. Auggh! Back to the bathroom for the inhaler, which I'd left there.

In my room again, I looked out the window, expecting to see Kristy crossing my lawn on her way back to my house. Instead, she was still in Mr. Finch's yard. She was standing with her back to me, bent over something near the end of the patio. When she stood up, I saw what it was. A garbage can. Kristy was going through Mr. Finch's garbage!

Then she held up something. At first I couldn't tell what it was. Then I focused my binoculars on it. "Oh, excellent," I whispered. It was more evidence; a partially burnt photo. Yes!

Just then, I heard another car. And I didn't even have to swing around my binoculars to see who it was.

It was Mr. Finch, pulling into his driveway.

I opened the window, then grabbed for the harmonica and started blowing like mad at Kristy. The good news was that she heard the harmonica . . . and the car. The bad news? I was a little too late. She was stuck. There was no way she could make it out of Mr. Finch's backyard without his seeing her. He'd already climbed out of his car, and he was heading for the back door.

CHAPTER 13

"Kristy!" I croaked. My throat had gone completely dry. "Oh my lord." I couldn't believe my eyes. Kristy was standing there like a deer caught in headlights as Mr. Finch walked toward her. He hadn't seen her yet, but he would — at any moment. Why, oh why couldn't he use his front door? Or even his side door, the one he was just about to walk past? Why did he insist on using that back door?

Kristy looked paralyzed, and I couldn't blame her. I don't know what I would have done in that situation. If she ran, he'd know she had been up to no good. If she stayed, she'd have to explain herself. And what could she possibly say?

Oh, what a mess. I was going to have to stand there at my window and watch one of my best friends come face-to-face with a criminal. And just because he wasn't wanted for murder or some other violent crime didn't mean he wasn't a bad guy. Who knew what he would do if he thought he was cornered? After all, this was a man who'd abandoned his family.

All of these thoughts came to me in about one and a half seconds, the time it took for Mr. Finch to cross part of the distance between his car and Kristy. Then, just in time, one more thought entered my groggy brain.

I jumped up and spun around. Sure enough, the phone was still lying on my bed. I grabbed it and hit the redial button. The phone would automatically dial the number Kristy had entered less than half an hour earlier.

I picked up the binoculars again and watched. Kristy's face still showed how terrified she felt. Mr. Finch's face was a blank — until he heard something. Then his eyes shifted toward the house and I could almost hear his thoughts. *Phone's ringing. Better answer it. Guess I'll use the side door.*

He reached out for the knob on the side door, which led through the garage to the house. Then he turned it and went inside. I almost melted with relief. I aimed the binoculars at Kristy and saw the panic disappear, replaced by a sly glance at my window, a little grin, and a thumbs-up sign. She waved the burned photo she'd found. Then she started to run — toward the other side of Mr. Finch's house.

"Hello?"

I almost dropped the phone. I'd forgotten I'd dialed it, and now Mr. Finch had answered. And he expected to hear someone on the other end. What was I going to say? I couldn't impersonate a phone company employee again. I had the feeling that Mr. Finch was probably already suspicious enough after that last phone call and the wild goose chase it had sent him on.

"Hello?" he asked again.

Almost on its own, my thumb snuck up and pressed the OFF button. The phone went dead.

I was still watching through the binoculars, so I could see the look on Mr. Finch's face. He looked — I guess *bewildered* would be the word. But not overly upset. He just put the phone back into its cradle and walked away, shaking his head.

Then he headed out the sliding doors onto the patio and looked around for a moment. Maybe he sensed something in the air, had some suspicion that all was not right. I don't know, and I never will. I watched his face closely through the binoculars, and when I saw his glance stop suddenly at one point, I swept them around to see what he was looking at.

Oops.

Kristy had left the lid off the garbage can.

What would Mr. Finch make of that? I

watched as he replaced the lid, after just a quick glance inside the can. After that, he looked around one more time — I pulled away from the window, just in case — and headed back inside. Had he noticed that one of the burned photos was missing from his garbage can? I crossed my fingers, hoping with all my heart that he had not.

Bang! The screen door downstairs slammed, and I jumped. I listened to the footsteps thumping up the stairs.

"Abby?"

"Right here," I said.

"Do you think he saw me?" Kristy asked with a smile. She was still breathing hard. "I took the long way around, just in case. I didn't want him to see me crossing your yard."

"Good plan," I said. "And no, I don't think he spotted you."

"That was you on the phone, wasn't it?" she asked. "That was brilliant."

I blushed again. "I can't believe it worked," I said. "But now he's more suspicious than ever."

"Well, he may be suspicious, but we're beyond that. We're sure now," she said, thrusting the partially burned picture into my hand.

I looked down at it. The edges were charred, but I could still see the image of a woman standing on a dock, with sunlight glinting off the water. She was tall, with curly blonde hair and a pleasant, smiling face. The same face I'd seen over and over again as I watched the *Mystery Trackers* video. It was Arthur Maguire's wife, the one who'd been featured in several photos that had flashed across the screen, as well as in the birthday party video. There was no question about it.

"It's her, isn't it?" I asked. "Mrs. Maguire."

"Definitely," said Kristy. "And those drawings? The one of a house was signed Patty. And the rocket ship —"

"— was by Joseph," I finished.

She nodded. "They were both signed in big, fat grade-school handwriting. I could read it perfectly from the window."

"Wow," I murmured. "It's really him."

"It really is," she agreed. "This is awesome."

"It's only awesome if they catch him," I reminded her. "I think it's time for another call to Sergeant Johnson."

Kristy agreed. "Let's do it now." She grabbed the phone from my bed and handed it to me.

I dialed and asked for Sergeant Johnson. I was connected right away. "Hi, it's Abby again," I said. "Please don't hang up!"

Sergeant Johnson laughed. "I wasn't about to," he said. "But I am pretty busy. What's up?"

"I know you told me you were on the case. But I just wanted to add one thing. Well, two."

I explained as quickly as I could about the names on the drawings. Then I went on, barely stopping for breath. "And second, there were these pictures he was burning in the sink, and we — um — we got our hands on one of them," I glanced at Kristy, "and it was of a woman. A woman who looks exactly like the pictures and video of Arthur Maguire's wife." I didn't mean to sound so dramatic, but that's how it came out.

"Okay, Abby," said Sergeant Johnson. "You know I appreciate the information. And I've already been in touch with the Des Moines police. They're faxing some photos over, and I may be paying a visit to your neighbor one day soon. But do me a favor. Keep this to yourselves for now. Understand?"

I nodded vigorously, then realized he couldn't see that over the phone. "I do," I said. "I promise. We won't tell a soul."

"And Abby?" he asked. "I don't know how you got those photos, and I'm not going to ask right now. But stay away from Mr. Finch. I mean that."

"I know," I said. "And I will. So will Kristy."

"This is in our hands now," he went on. "If you just lie low for a couple of days, everything will be taken care of."

CHAPTER 14

Tuesday

Go, sped racer, go! Wasn't that a blast today, waching our charges racing there go carts? And they had fun too. Abby you should have seen it. The only thing I'm still curiose about is how Kristy knew about a team none of the rest of us had ever herd of....

I didn't go to the go-cart races on Tuesday afternoon, partly because I was still feeling pretty tired and partly — yes, I admit it — because I wanted to keep an eye on Mr. Finch. I was keeping my promise to Sergeant Johnson. I wasn't going anywhere near Mr. Finch's house. But I couldn't resist watching him through my binoculars. It had become a habit.

So I had to find out about the races from my friends and from reading Claudia's entry in the club notebook. On the afternoon of the race, she was sitting for Jamie and Lucy Newton, two of our favorite charges. Jamie's four, very smart and very sweet. His baby sister, Lucy, is a charmer too. She can deliver a beautiful smile even though all her teeth aren't in yet.

"Claudee!" Jamie shouted as Claudia hurried up the Newtons' front walk. He flung himself into her arms. "I've been waiting for you. Can we go see the races? Please? Mommy says it's okay, as long as you want to go. Do you want to go? Do you?" Jamie was tugging on Claudia's pant leg. (She was wearing a super-baggy pair of painter's pants, customized with wild embroidery she'd done herself.)

Claudia laughed, and as soon as Jamie stopped for a breath she told him she'd be glad to take him and his little sister.

"Yea!" he yelled. "I want to ride my bike,

okay? And Lucy can go in her stroller."

"Sounds good to me," said Claudia. "Should we make your bike and her stroller look extra fancy for the occasion?"

Jamie was thrilled at this idea and could hardly contain himself. Just then, Mrs. Newton stepped onto the porch, holding Lucy. "I hope you don't mind taking them to the races," she told Claudia, apologetically, as she handed over the baby.

"No problem," said Claudia. "I was hoping to go anyway."

As soon as Mrs. Newton had driven away, Claudia sat Lucy in her baby seat and began to take things out of her Kid-Kit. "We can use some of this construction paper and a few of these stickers," she told Jamie. "Your bike will look totally cool."

Once the bike and stroller were decorated (an activity Claudia had suggested in order to use up some time, since she knew the race didn't start until four-thirty), it was time to head out. The race route was on the part of Burnt Hill Road that swoops past Carle Playground, one of Jamie's favorite spots to play.

Claudia pushed the stroller while Jamie rode his bike (which is still equipped with training wheels) slowly down the sidewalk. As they approached the playground, they could see that quite a crowd had gathered near the starting line, at the top of the hill. A police car with its lights flashing stood near the starting line, blocking traffic from going down the hill.

Jamie whooped. "Cool!" he shouted. Lucy, in her stroller, let out a squeal of happiness. Jamie's excitement was contagious.

When they arrived at the playground, they saw that all the teams were on hand. Each go-cart had to be checked by the officials running the race, and while the kids waited their turns they worked feverishly, putting final touches on their go-carts.

"Hey, Claudia!" Claud turned to see Jessi waving at her. She and Mary Anne were standing near the Glory Girls' go-cart. Charlotte, wearing a helmet, was the driver, and she was showing off the team's creation. "See, we made it so you can steer even if the go-cart is going backward," she said.

"Brilliant," said Jessi.

Mary Anne coughed and nodded her head toward the Rodowskys' bright orange go-cart, which stood nearby. The steering mechanism looked awfully familiar.

"Oh, well," Jessi said softly. "They say imitation is the best form of flattery."

"And where did you come up with the idea for this special foot brake?" Claudia asked the girls. She had a feeling she knew, since there was a similar part on the Rodowskys' go-cart.

There was an embarrassed silence.

Jamie broke it, calling to Claudia. "Come on," he said. "Let's go see the triplets' go-cart. It looks really neat." He pointed toward a purple go-cart with a crowd of kids hovering around it.

As they drew closer, Claudia saw that the team's name was painted across the side of the go-cart.

"What does that say?" Jamie asked.

" 'The Fleet Four,' " Claudia read for him. "Interesting. I thought their name was The Speedy Three." Then she spotted a small figure in a bike helmet. "Nicky?" she asked. "What's up?"

"I'm the driver!" he cried, smiling happily. Then he bent over the go-cart to check one of the wheels.

Claudia saw Stacey and Mal standing nearby and gave them a quizzical glance. "How did this happen?" she asked. She knew, from reading their notes, that something big had changed if Nicky was not only on the triplets' team but had become their driver.

"See those cool decals?" asked Mal, pointing to the go-cart. "They're one-of-a-kind, and they were part of Nicky's collection. The triplets decided they *had* to have them — and Nicky knew how to drive a hard bargain."

Everybody cracked up. Score one for Nicky!

Then there was a screeching sound, and some static. "Ladies and gentlemen, boys and girls," an announcement boomed over the portable PA system. "It's time for the races to begin. Will all teams please bring their go-carts to the starting line?"

As the kids pushed and pulled their go-carts to the area marked off by yellow ropes, the announcer explained how the race was going to work. Each go-cart would roll down the hill in turn, while two timers checked the speed with stopwatches. The prize money would be donated to the winning team's designated charity. "Additional contributions to any of the charities are welcome, and we've set up a table to take them," the announcer finished, gesturing toward a table near the starting line. "And now, welcome to the First Annual Stoneybrook Community Center Go-cart Races!"

The kids lined up to take their turns, talking excitedly. And the sitters? They were pretty excited too. Mal was rooting for the triplets' team, now that they'd let Nicky be a part of it. Jessi and Mary Anne were sure that the Glory Girls were going to win. And Stacey and Claudia were for the Rodowsky boys. They were just crossing their fingers and hoping that the go-cart would make it to the finish line in one piece, with Jackie at the wheel.

Several other teams were participating too,

119

made up of kids none of the BSC members knew very well. All the go-carts looked excellent, and Claudia admired the creativity that had gone into building them.

The races began. There were three heats, so each team had three chances to produce a winning time.

In between runs, Claudia began to wonder about something. "Where's Kristy?" she asked. Nobody knew.

As each team took its turn, the crowd cheered wildly. The runs were getting faster and faster as the drivers learned the course. "Looking good, Jackie!" Claudia yelled as Jackie crossed the finish line in a blur of speed. "We can't be beat," she said to Stacey in a lower voice. "This race is all sewed up." And it looked as if she were right. No other team was nearly as fast.

Then, suddenly, one more go-cart appeared on the scene. It was the Korman kids, Bill and Melody — with Kristy! "Are we too late?" she asked, panting. She conferred with the judges and must have convinced them to let the Kormans race, because soon Melody was donning a helmet and lowering herself into the go-cart.

"Uh-oh," said Claudia, eyeing the go-cart, which looked long and low and very, very fast. "I have a feeling these guys might give us some competition."

She was right. The Kormans' go-cart was much faster than any of the others that day.

Kristy grinned when first prize was announced. Bill and Melody had chosen to give their prize money to a shelter for homeless people, which Kristy thought was a great choice. She was thrilled that they'd won. But she never let on how she'd learned about their "secret" go-cart.

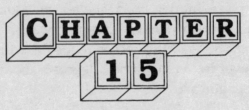

CHAPTER 15

"Y̲ou look as if you're feeling better, Abby." Mary Anne smiled at me. "It will be great to have you back at school."

I smiled back. "Thanks. I am feeling better, finally. I may even be able to make it to school — and to our meeting! — on Friday."

"Cool," said Kristy absently. She was staring out the window at Mr. Finch's house.

Every member of the BSC was in my room, paying me a special visit before Wednesday's meeting. I was feeling much, much better, although I still didn't have the energy to make it over to Claudia's. So the club had come to me.

"Kristy, what are you looking at?" asked Jessi.

"Not much," Kristy admitted. She turned to look at me. "Have the shades been like that for long?" she asked.

"All day," I told her. I'd been keeping tabs on

Mr. Finch since I woke up, but I hadn't had a glimpse of him yet. Why? Because his shades were drawn, and they had been since morning. What was going on over there? I was dying of curiosity.

"So far, spying seems kind of boring," Stacey pointed out. "I thought you guys might be on the verge of catching a real criminal. But if this is what you've been looking at all this time, I can't say I'm envious." She stifled a yawn.

Kristy and I looked at each other and smiled. We both knew how exciting — and addicting — spying on the neighbors could be. But we didn't expect our friends to understand. And, since Sergeant Johnson had sworn us to secrecy, we hadn't even told them about all the latest developments.

"Tell me more about the go-cart races," I said, to change the subject. Not that I could think about much besides Mr. Finch, and what might happen next. Were the police ever going to show up? Was Sergeant Johnson just humoring me, or was he really on the case? I was dying to call him again, but I knew he'd probably just tell me to butt out, though he'd find a much more polite way to say it.

". . . . was awesome," Claudia was saying.

I'd tuned out the first part of what she'd said, but I knew she must be talking about the Kormans' go-cart.

"I know," I said without thinking. "I had a feeling that go-cart would be fast."

Claudia gave me a strange look. "You *what*?" she asked.

Oops. "Um, I mean, from what you've been telling me," I said. It was too embarrassing to admit just how much time I'd spent watching my neighbors over the last week. And I knew Kristy had enjoyed being mysterious about the Kormans.

"Abby!"

I turned to see Kristy waving a hand at me as she continued to stare out the window. Something in her voice made me jump up and hurry to her side.

"What is it?" I asked.

"Look," she said, pointing. I looked, but at first I didn't see anything different. Mr. Finch's shades were still drawn, and the house seemed quiet. Then I noticed something. Mr. Finch's car was standing in the driveway, as it had been all morning. But now its trunk was open.

"He just came out and put a box in there," Kristy told me. "What do you think is going on?"

Before I could answer, the back door opened and Mr. Finch emerged, lugging a huge suitcase.

Kristy and I looked at each other, wide-eyed. "I don't believe it," she said.

"What? What's going on?" asked Claudia. She and the others crowded around the window in order to peer out.

"Is he going on a trip?" asked Mal.

"I don't know," I answered, "but I don't like the look of this." I ran for the phone and dialed Sergeant Johnson. I didn't care if he thought I was a pest. If Mr. Finch escaped, it wasn't going to be my fault.

"Sergeant Johnson, please?" Holding the phone to my ear, I walked to the window. Mr. Finch had stuffed the suitcase into the trunk of the car and had gone back inside.

"I'm sorry," said the officer answering the phone at the station. "He isn't here right now. Can I take a message?"

"Can you ask him to call Abigail Stevenson?" I asked, figuring my full name sounded more impressive. I gave the officer my number and hung up. Then I watched hopelessly as Mr. Finch loaded another box into his car.

"What are we going to do?" I asked Kristy.

"I'm thinking, I'm thinking," she said.

The other club members stood watching. "I don't know what's going on," said Stacey, "but I have the feeling Mr. Finch may be history soon."

"And there's nothing we can do about it," I said. "Is there?" Maybe Kristy had come up with some brainstorm.

She shook her head. "Not without putting ourselves in danger," she said. "And we made a promise to Sergeant Johnson about that."

Just then, I spotted movement out of the corner of my eye. It was a car, driving slowly up Mr. Finch's street. Another car cruised slowly in the opposite direction. "Wait a second," I said, not daring to hope. I ran for the binoculars. "It's them!" I yelled.

"Who?" asked Jessi. "The cavalry?"

She was joking, but in a way she was right. This moment was just like the ones in those old westerns when the cavalry comes charging over the hill at the last minute to save the day.

"Even better," I said. "Sergeant Johnson is here. And I think that paper he's holding might just be a warrant for a certain person's arrest."

That was the moment when everything started happening at once. Sergeant Johnson climbed out of his unmarked detective's car, and two other police officers climbed out of the other car. Both were now parked in front of Mr. Finch's house. At the same time, Mr. Finch emerged from his house, carrying another box. When he saw the men coming up his walk, he dropped the box and stood there for a second, as if he were paralyzed. I focused the binoculars on his face and saw that he was panicked.

Just then, three police cars roared up the street, sirens blaring. Another one came up my street, as if to cut off any escape route.

"Whoa!" whispered Claudia.

"Is he going to put up a fight?" Kristy wondered.

He didn't. Instead, he put up his hands.

Sergeant Johnson walked right up to him and showed him the paper he was holding. Then one of the other officers snapped a pair of handcuffs onto Mr. Finch's wrists, while Sergeant Johnson talked to him. I've watched enough police dramas to guess what he was saying. "You have the right to remain silent . . ."

Just then, bright lights lit up the scene. "What's happening?" cried Stacey.

I swept the binoculars around until I caught sight of the TV cameras. "It must be *Mystery Trackers*," I said. "I bet they're filming the arrest."

I will *never* forget that day. It was one of the most thrilling events of my life. After the police took Mr. Finch away, Kristy and I told our friends everything that had happened over the last few days. Then they all took off for the BSC meeting, leaving me to "rest." Of course I couldn't; I was way too excited. I could hardly wait to tell my mom and Anna about Mr. Finch. So far, they thought his greatest crime was mowing his lawn too early in the morning!

But before they came home I had two incredible phone calls. One was from Sergeant Johnson, congratulating me on breaking the case. "You did it, Abby," he said. "I didn't believe you at first, but you were right all along. Congratulations."

He went on to tell me that Mr. Finch would be sent back to Iowa, where he'd be tried and sentenced for his crimes. Sergeant Johnson made sure to add that the Maguire family was doing fine. "From what the Des Moines police told me, the community out there is taking good care of them," he said. "The kids will be okay." He knew I'd been worried about that.

The other call was from Amy Shapiro. She had heard about the arrest and she was bubbling over with enthusiasm. "Great work, Abby," she cried. "You know, that's the first successful arrest they've filmed since I started working here!"

I congratulated her. "You were part of this too, you know," I told her. "Without your encouragement, I might not have followed up on the case."

"Thanks for saying so," she said. "I'm trying hard to prove to my bosses that I deserve a full-time job here after my internship is up, and this case is going to go a long way toward convincing them. But most of the credit for this arrest goes to you. And *all* the reward money. The check is already in the mail."

Reward? I could hardly believe my ears.

Cool. Maybe I'd buy myself a *really* good pair of binoculars. Or, maybe not. What were the chances of catching another criminal in my very own neighborhood? Maybe I'd just take my friends out for pizza, instead.

L. GODWIN

Ann M. Martin

About the Author

ANN MATTHEWS MARTIN was born on August 12, 1955. She grew up in Princeton, NJ, with her parents and her younger sister, Jane.

Although Ann used to be a teacher and then an editor of children's books, she's now a full-time writer. She gets ideas for her books from many different places. Some are based on personal experiences. Others are based on childhood memories and feelings. Many are written about contemporary problems or events.

All of Ann's characters, even the members of the Baby-sitters Club, are made up. (So is Stoneybrook.) But many of her characters are based on real people. Sometimes Ann names her characters after people she knows, other times she chooses names she likes.

In addition to the Baby-sitters Club books, Ann Martin has written many other books for children. Her favorite is *Ten Kids, No Pets* because she loves big families and she loves animals. Her favorite Baby-sitters Club book is *Kristy's Big Day*. (By the way, Kristy is her favorite baby-sitter!)

Ann M. Martin now lives in New York with her cats, Gussie, Woody, and Willy. Her hobbies are reading, sewing, and needlework — especially making clothes for children.

Look for Mystery #36

KRISTY AND THE CAT BURGLAR

We walked down the driveway, which wound through the woods. Suddenly it opened out into a large clearing. In the middle of the clearing stood an impressive stone house. It looked almost like an old castle, with ivy crawling all over it and dozens of leaded-glass windows. Nobody was stirring, and I didn't see any cars or other signs of life. There was something almost creepy about the place, especially now that the sun was starting to go down.

"Okay, we've seen it," I said. "Now it's time to go home."

"But —" Karen began.

Just then, a shot rang out.

Really! I know it sounds dramatic, but that's exactly what happened. And even though I haven't heard too many actual gunshots in my life, somehow I was pretty sure that's what I was hearing now.

"Let's go!" I said. "Now!" I grabbed Karen with one hand and David Michael with the other, and we started to run toward the road. Fast.

Suddenly, a loud siren began to wail. Bright lights snapped on, illuminating the entire clearing. I felt totally exposed.

I ran even faster. Something was happening at that house, and I didn't want to be any part of it. All those alarms going off — was that because we'd walked too near the house? Or was it something more serious?

Then I heard another high wail — the sound of police sirens. They were coming closer by the second. Then the sirens stopped. I heard slamming doors and voices. I tightened my hold on Karen and David Michael and pulled them down the driveway. All I wanted was to get out of there.

We were nearing the stone wall, the road beyond it, and safety. We passed the mailbox, and I had just begun to loosen my grip, when suddenly a voice rang out behind us.

"DON'T MOVE!"

Read all the books
about **Abby**
in the Baby-sitters Club series
by Ann M. Martin

Portrait Collection:

Abby's Book
> Abby tells about the tragedies and comedies of her up-and-down life.

THE BABY-SITTERS CLUB®

by Ann M. Martin

Collect and read these exciting BSC Super Specials, Mysteries, and Super Mysteries along with your favorite Baby-sitters Club books!

BSC Super Specials

❑ BBK44240-6	Baby-sitters on Board! Super Special #1	$3.95
❑ BBK44239-2	Baby-sitters' Summer Vacation Super Special #2	$3.95
❑ BBK43973-1	Baby-sitters' Winter Vacation Super Special #3	$3.95
❑ BBK42493-9	Baby-sitters' Island Adventure Super Special #4	$3.95
❑ BBK43575-2	California Girls! Super Special #5	$3.95
❑ BBK43576-0	New York, New York! Super Special #6	$4.50
❑ BBK44963-X	Snowbound! Super Special #7	$3.95
❑ BBK44962-X	Baby-sitters at Shadow Lake Super Special #8	$3.95
❑ BBK45661-X	Starring The Baby-sitters Club! Super Special #9	$3.95
❑ BBK45674-1	Sea City, Here We Come! Super Special #10	$3.95
❑ BBK47015-9	The Baby-sitters Remember Super Special #11	$3.95
❑ BBK48308-0	Here Come the Bridesmaids! Super Special #12	$3.95
❑ BBK22883-8	Aloha, Baby-sitters! Super Special #13	$4.50
❑ BBK69126-X	BSC in the USA Super Special #14	$4.50

BSC Mysteries

❑ BAI44084-5	#1 Stacey and the Missing Ring	$3.50
❑ BAI44085-3	#2 Beware Dawn!	$3.50
❑ BAI44799-8	#3 Mallory and the Ghost Cat	$3.50
❑ BAI44800-5	#4 Kristy and the Missing Child	$3.50
❑ BAI44801-3	#5 Mary Anne and the Secret in the Attic	$3.50
❑ BAI44961-3	#6 The Mystery at Claudia's House	$3.50
❑ BAI44960-5	#7 Dawn and the Disappearing Dogs	$3.50
❑ BAI44959-1	#8 Jessi and the Jewel Thieves	$3.50
❑ BAI44958-3	#9 Kristy and the Haunted Mansion	$3.50
❑ BAI45696-2	#10 Stacey and the Mystery Money	$3.50

More titles ➡

The Baby-sitters Club books continued...

BSC Super Mysteries

Available wherever you buy books...or use this order form.

Scholastic Inc., P.O. Box 7502, 2931 East McCarty Street, Jefferson City, MO 65102-7502

Please send me the books I have checked above. I am enclosing $ _____
(please add $2.00 to cover shipping and handling). Send check or money order
— no cash or C.O.D.s please.

Name_____Birthdate_____

Address _____

City_____State/Zip_____